Freelon Starbird

Freelon Starbird

Being a Narrative of the Extraordinary
Hardships Suffered by an Accidental Soldier
in a Beaten Army
During the Autumn and Winter of 1776

RICHARD F. SNOW

Illustrated by Ben F. Stahl

Houghton Mifflin Company Boston 1976

Library of Congress Cataloging in Publication Data

Snow, Richard F
  Freelon Starbird.

  SUMMARY: A reluctant young patriot describes his
experiences in the Revolutionary Army after waking following a night of drinking to the disturbing recollection
of having signed up the night before to fight the British.
  [1. United States—History—Revolution, 1775–1783—
Fiction] I. Stahl, Ben F. II. Title.
PZ7.S68513Fr   [Fic]   75-43901
ISBN 0-395-24275-4

v 10 9 8 7 6 5 4 3 2 1

For my mother and father

It is said all martyrdoms looked mean
when they were suffered.

Emerson

Freelon Starbird

1

Polly Lycott

My name is Freelon Starbird.

I bore arms as a soldier in our great war for independence, and, though I joined the ranks through the worst kind of folly and never went anywhere with the army but I wished I were somewhere else, I now find there are certain things I would like to say about my service. More and more these days I hear brave and nonsensical stories about the American colonies, Thirteen Sisters by the Sea, who slumbered awhile in Liberty's cradle until with fierce and common purpose they rose and girded on armor against the thunderbolts of British tyranny. Men left the plow in the field and the shop untended, banded together, and, when the hirelings of King George came against them, they knelt behind walls and fences and gave them a fine drubbing, as God himself had ordained.

Now, these are splendid stories, but nothing I knew, and they nettle me; for if the American Revolution was so sure to end victorious, then it seems to me that I passed some miserable hours to little purpose. I have begun to worry that, when I and the others who fought in that war are dead and gone, we will be remembered as fortunate men who took part in the grandest, pleasantest pageant in all the world. It was not that, but rather a sort of horrible, sickly task where all went wrong that could go wrong, and any part of a man's body that could pain him did.

I have come to try to write truly of what happened to me and to those with whom I served. And I confide that the events I here chronicle will do the past no more dishonor than the silly tales of British regiments fleeing like rabbits whenever they brushed up against farmers in homespun.

I was not a farmer in homespun, but a watchmaker in broadcloth. I was a watchmaker because my father was a watchmaker. He was an extremely good one, and I, in those days before the war, was on the way to becoming well skilled myself. I was less pleased about this than my father because, while he was able to manipulate tiny cogs and collets in his handsome shop, I was given such dismal chores as befit an apprentice. Mankind, in its long progress toward civilization, has never been able to devise more tedious a task than resilvering the dial of a clock. So I spent my days dissolving lunar caustic in rainwater, stirring in table salt and cream of tartar, and working the resultant paste into clock dials while great events took place about me in Philadelphia. But they did not seem great to me at the time, or even of any particular interest, for I, like most twenty-year-olds, was infatuated.

The object of my ardor was a straw-haired girl named Polly Lycott, and my passion for her may have rested on no firmer a pedestal than the fact that she laughed long and emptily at all my attempts at wit. Be that as it may, it was enough for somebody barely out of his adolescence, and I was enraptured.

I was, of course, aware of the war that was gathering momentum up to the north, but it seemed a pallid business compared to my pursuit of the lovely Polly. Nevertheless, almost from the outset small events conspired to prod me toward the conflict.

Every now and again, once I had become a soldier, I would look back on the previous months in hopes of determining when I first set foot on the path that led to my miserable situation, and usually I thought of a hot day in September of 1775.

On that Saturday I was making my way back to the shop from the printer with some watch papers he had made up for us. They were handsome ones, I recall, showing Time and Death engaged in a mournful dialogue beside a sundial, with the legend "Jno. Starbird, Clocks and Watches" floating magically in the sky above them. I was exasperated from a long and unusually stupid conversation with the printer, who had read that the color black attracted the heat, and was delighted with the possibility of painting an egg black and thereby roasting it in the sun.

I was toiling along thinking of eggs and watch papers when I saw Polly's bright head coming toward me down Second Street through the swarming September sunlight. She spied me at the same instant, stopped before me, and said, "Why, Freelon, you look terribly glum and thoughtful."

"No, no!" I cried, feeling, as always, that I was startling her a little with my enthusiasm. "It's a splendid surprise to see you. I trust that all is well?"

"Yes, it is," she said, and then added, to my great displeasure, "for I have been having a most interesting discussion with Sligo Consett." Consett was the son of a deacon, a gloomy hypocrite with a high, whiny voice. Of all my acquaintances, Polly alone liked him. But this, God knows, did not make me like him any better.

"Are you quite sure it was Consett?" I replied nastily. "For I never knew him to be capable of an interesting discussion."

"Oh, Freelon," she said, "I cannot imagine why you are so cruel to him. He is very sensible, and he never has a bad word to say about you."

Of course not, I thought, since he is such a pious prig. I was sure he never had a bad word to say about anybody, although he occasionally expressed concern about the state of people's immortal souls. I realized that it would be a mistake to say any of this to Polly and then remembered the fact that Consett, in his fastidious way, was calmly and primly loyal to the king.

"He is a Tory coward," I said, "who does not give any consideration to these critical times."

With the sort of tact that would doubtless have made

4

my life a misery had I ever won her, Polly laughed in my face and demanded to know when I had given the faintest consideration to any critical times. This was true enough, but I had already committed myself, and so I pressed on. I groped about for something to say and began, I am afraid, to talk in newspaper terms about "the effusion of blood by brave men pledged to stand against the arbitrary demands of tyrants." On I went, speaking of myself as though I were a grim crusader. Polly was amused at first and then almost immediately bored. She peered about at the crowds come to market until I brought her attention back toward me by barking out something about "that damned fat King George."

The effect of this bold statement was not at all what I had hoped, however, for it was overheard by a man who was shopping for butter nearby. He had been tasting a scraping that he had taken with a coin from a merchant's small pyramid of the stuff. Upon hearing me, he turned around, thrust the coin back into a pocket, and walked briskly over to me.

"Do I have the honor of addressing Mr. Samuel Adams?" he demanded.

"You do not, sir," I answered quite civilly, for he was very large and, although grinning pleasantly, made me wary.

"Well, whoever you may be, I am pleased to hear a son of liberty speaking so bravely on the matters of the day."

I smiled in acknowledgment and he smiled down at me and it was most uncomfortable and wrong.

5

"And, sir," he continued with his smile and his small black eyes moving quickly between me and Polly, "were you indicating to this young woman" — he made a slight bow toward Polly, who looked demurely at her shoes — "that you will soon be fighting fat King George's troops?"

"That, sir, is my intention," I replied, although it was not at all and had never been my intention.

"Then," he said cheerfully, "you may wish to begin by fighting me, you nose-grooming faggot-porter."

He stood there, big as a tree and perfectly at ease, and I realized that there would be no dignified way out of this except by fighting him, which I was wholly unwilling to do. I have always been a wretched fighter, and even had I been a good one this monster could easily have settled the issue by sitting on me. On the other hand, there was Polly next to me. I stood dumbstruck, wondering in my confusion whether to strike a feeble blow at him and count on passers-by to intercede before he could do me any real harm. Polly began to giggle, and the smile on my challenger's face grew into a fierce toothy grimace.

"Well, then," he said in his bantering way, "I am dismayed to see that I have enraged and astounded you with my impertinence in addressing you in such a manner." I stammered something — I cannot imagine what — and he leaned toward me. "What? What did you say?"

"Nothing," I replied miserably, "for I have no wish to fight you."

"Oh, I can see that readily enough. I'm tired of hearing lickspittles like you cawing away against our sovereign. Go join your precious Washington in the field — you'll do him no good, his enemies no harm, and you may well give me no small pleasure by stopping a ball. Good afternoon, sir; my apologies for intruding upon your conversation, ma'am." And at last he turned away and went back to the butter stall.

"Poor Freelon," said Polly. "But it serves you right for acting such a son of Mars."

"Well," I said, angry and humiliated, "it's easy enough to make a man look a fool if you take him by surprise, but my reluctance to take part in a brawl on Second Street doesn't mean that I can't use a musket if need arise."

"Oh, Freelon, such talk. Now, there's no reason in the world for you to get involved in this rebellion. Sligo Consett says that bloodshed only begets more bloodshed and makes people unhappy, and that there should be more accord between people."

"Does Consett say that?" I replied. "I had no idea that Sligo was such a philosopher king. In fact, I'm sure so original an idea could not have been conceived by his feeble . . ."

Polly had been scowling at this, and now she spoke: "It is much too fine a day to have to listen to your silly, hateful prattle. Good-bye, Freelon; I'm sure you'll bring back a brace of Hessians, so long as they don't frighten you by talking to you before the battle." She turned away from me and took her blond self into the crowds and out of sight.

Shaken and disgusted with myself, I made my way

7

home, mulling over clever remarks that I could have made to the beefy Tory and realizing all the while that any such remarks would have gotten my ears cuffed. I entered my father's shop in a poisonous mood, to which he added by demanding why my errand had taken so long. I threw the bundle of watch papers on the counter before him and started sullenly toward the door, which he interpreted rightly enough as insolence.

"Come here, sir!" he said, and I did so.

My father was as tidy and compacted as one of his watches, a small, immaculate man who had conquered what he claimed to have been a ferocious temper by working out a good watchmaker's philosophy. Over the years he had come to see himself as one who dealt in the passing of life itself. All those tiny gold deaths swinging their scythes on the dials of his more complicated timepieces had entered his very spirit. On the wall of his shop there hung an engraving of Queen Elizabeth in old age, gaunt but still an object of awesome if eroded power. Flanking the Virgin Queen, older, gaunter, and more powerful still, a weary and smiling Death leaned over a large clock of antique design, waiting. A pace or so behind Death there stood a wholly inexplicable third figure, an unremarkable man in court costume attending not, as good courtiers should, to his Queen but rather to her shadowy companion. Whomever this man may have been meant to represent, I am sure that my father felt it was himself, a calm secretary to the Grim Reaper. The tiny whirrings and chitterings that surrounded him in his shop were to him a constant reminder of the machineries of life ticking their way toward the grave. It was, he felt, his calling to dispense this sad information to the gentry, who might make use of it as they wished, but who were nonetheless reminded by his efforts that the time they had to devote to their various pursuits was not limitless. My father, in consequence, saw little but futility in attempts to alter the course of things; content came to a man merely in the markings of their passage. It was, to a young man, a tiresome philosophy, but one that kept me from being the recipient of too many beatings in my youth.

Now, as usual, my father seemed more curious than nettled. "Freelon," he said, setting down a gear in a small phial of liquid, "may I ask what is disturbing you?"

Having no inclination to discuss Polly or my recent embarrassment, I clung to the luckless story about my interest in the rebellion. "As you may know, Father, these are weighty times," I proclaimed, "and I have been trying to decide whether or not my place is in the field . . ."

"Oh," he said, tweezing the gear out of the phial and putting it into another one, "I would have thought it was because you had a squabble with Polly Lycott."

I had been given little reason to expect success with my stories this day, but this last from my father truly astonished me, for I had always thought that the doings of myself and my friends were as obscure to him as the transactions of a group of chipmunks. Moreover, I had not spoken of Polly in his hearing ever since he had, a year ago, enraged me by casually remarking that "the vapid little thing" seemed to have a certain slight charm.

"Excuse me, Freelon," he said. "I do not bring this up to taunt you, but because I am concerned to think of you becoming a soldier. I know that it is distressing to fight with a girl, but it is not worth going to the grave for; you'll not meet other girls there.

"And this war, Freelon, is no struggle of ours. We are not wretched or oppressed; we need no violent upheaval in order to survive. We are moderately prosperous people in a prosperous city in a prosperous colony. All the colonies prosper. This talk about our rights is all philosophy, and philosophies are very flimsy constructions. It seems the most wanton foolishness to spill blood for such an abstraction. If the philosophy is a good one, it will come to pass in due course, and if it's not, it is surely not worthwhile losing a leg for."

I had heard this from my father before. He was probably the least ardent loyalist in the colonies. He had no belief in the divine right of kings and no particular interest in England, but he did have an abiding love of order, and the idea of a group of political philosophers backed up by an army of farmers bringing chaos down upon him and his watches appalled him.

"Moreover," he went on, "it's a war that cannot be won. Britain does not want to let us go, nor does she have to. She has a real army — not a crowd of shop-clerks with muskets they barely know how to use. She has a navy, and we're all coast, from north to south, so she can put her army wherever she pleases. The English can go where they like and strike where they like, and there isn't a ship in the colonies that could stand in the way of one of the king's frigates, let alone one of his three-deckers."

Here was the practical extension of his faith in the slow evolutions of an orderly system. He was probably right enough, but, although I had not hitherto given serious consideration to fighting the English, the project did have a gleam for me. I was young and had been well fired the evening, half a year before, when Iz Bissel came clattering into the city with the news of Lexington and Concord.

We had congregated in the smoke and noise of the King of Prussia Tavern and, amid much ale and with odd self-congratulation, absorbed the story of the long-anticipated definite act. It was a brightly colored tale, filled with detail and, most likely, lies. Here came clouds of British infantry to bulwark some obnoxious royal policy or governor's decree, falling on an innocent town, firing dwellings, shooting honest tradesmen who wished only to protect their merchandise and livelihoods, plundering taverns, but tarrying too long. And here came the Americans (I suspect the militia were not called by that name that evening, but somehow it has lodged in my mind as a piece of the drama) at the summons of churchbells and bloody-spurred riders. There was pitched battle at a certain bridge, and the cowards broke and fled, pursued by men who were congealing into an avenging army even as they chased their tormentors back into Boston. Now they were waiting, grim and silent, on the heights above the harbor, and the city was besieged.

Now, this was heady stuff. I went home filled with

11

cordial waters and plans, and woke the next morning muzzily thinking of New England.

I had never been to New England; it was far off and there was little there I wished to see. We sometimes had New Englanders in our shop. In fact, one appeared that very day while I was fumbling with a crude wooden clockwork. He was like the others, so far as I could tell — smug, high-voiced, and displeased that he was no longer in New England. Prices here were exorbitant. Our stock was pathetic. In Boston, not a month before, he had seen a clock of such wonderful ingenuity that, on the hour, a tiny silver man ran out of a tiny silver house and swung an ax against a tiny silver tree. There was nothing like that in Philadelphia, even though it was the second largest city in the British Empire. And off he went, delighted with being from New England and even more offensive than a visiting Frenchman. And there were the Yankee peddlers, half-legend even in my youth, who would sing the silver out of your purse and leave you holding a soiled piece of string or a smudged card with the days of the week printed on it for your edification.

So I began at once to draw back from battle, feeling that if these supernaturally self-contented people had touched off a war with Britain, then they were welcome to handle it on their own without taking me away from Polly. Hours before, I had longed to stand with bold companions on the field of victory, holding my musket and showing my teeth, but the combination of remorse and amorousness that comes after a night of drinking had whittled my ambition down to a small and pleasant longing merely to sit with Polly in a leafy place by the Schuylkill. Why should I fight New England's war? This temperate resolve not to mix in a neighbor's quarrels was leavened, I suspect, by memories of my uncle's description of his service. He had been to Ticonderoga on Abercromby's hideously ill managed campaign during the war against the French twenty years earlier, and never was a man more willing to decry the glories of battle.

"Quebec!" he'd snort over his claret when Wolfe's great victory was mentioned at our table. "I've heard enough of Quebec. You should have seen the log wall of Ticonderoga. Everybody bloody and screeching and the dead hanging in the branches like scarecrows, and those of us who had legs left nearly running them off to get away. God damn it, no commander got killed in *that* battle; Montcalm was behind a wall, and Abercromby a mile away. If I ever pick up my musket again, it'll be to prop open a door."

My uncle was a bitter man. He was, however, quite successful in land speculation, and his bitterness was tied to a noisy jocularity. He was rough and volatile, and, though I believe he was fond of my steady father, he delighted in making him nervous. This he did exceedingly well. In its lesser form this merely involved talking dangerously on controversial issues in the privacy of our home. But he could cause my father real anguish by walking with him in a public place and gripping his arm while making disgusting remarks to everybody who passed by.

After one such performance, as we were closing up

13

the shop and taking the more valuable watches upstairs, my father began to talk about my uncle. He said that, while one might be tempted to dismiss him as a coarse buffoon, such was not the case. My uncle had prospered through the carelessness of people who regarded him in that light. But the desire for wealth had not played any part in the development of his obnoxious character. It seemed, rather, that he had come by his bumptious ways under the spur of grief.

"We went to gatherings together, years ago," my father told me, "and I went in his shadow. He was courtly and gallant, and it was grand to be with him. There was a time when he could have had any woman in the city for the asking."

The woman he had asked, as it turned out, was one my father regarded with a caution that bordered on fear. She bore the unremarkable name of Sally Cooper and had been raised in a clan of pious folks who must have been relieved indeed when so presentable a citizen as Jonas Starbird won her hand. For Sally was a strange and random girl, lovely by all accounts, but filled with curious moods. At first she had admirers enough, but late or soon some swain would irritate her; she would respond with a savage remark, and he would leave to seek someone more manageable. Finally she had swept the field, leaving only my uncle, battered and grinning still, waiting there for her. So he had her at last. There was much fussing, I understand, from all quarters of our family, which my uncle weathered with the same offhand charm he brought to all his early endeavors.

As for Sally, she made him a splendid wife. She still made the family uncomfortable. She was still quick, random, and tart, but she leaned toward my uncle in any room, be it ever so wide, and he adored her. She, in turn, spared him the worst of her tempers, never insulted too worthy an acquaintance, watched over his house with the ferocious attention of an innkeeper's wife, and tried to bear him a child. But she was too frail for that task, and she died, and the child with her.

For a long time my uncle did nothing at all. When his friends offered their regrets, he was graceful about it, and when various of the Coopers wept, tears were not far from his eyes. But as the sad months bore Sally farther and farther from him, the old burr came into his character. He too became random and sharp, but in a coarse way that his intimates found alarming and finally revolting. At length he dropped all his old friends, pursued his own course, made new friends whom crasser men than my father found distasteful, and finally detached himself forever from his sometime orbit. He prospered, almost despite himself, squandered the profits in outrageous wagers, mocked his own ribaldry, and, in the main, kept his own company.

There was, to be sure, no sense of an old pain about him; his bumptiousness seemed real enough, as did his cheerful lack of sympathy for any human dilemma. Yet, when my mother fell sick of a fever at a time when my father had little money, my uncle paid a considerable sum to bring down from Boston a renowned physician. He did not consult my father on this and, after he had sent the man around to our house, insisted that he had called him down to Philadelphia to look after an ailment of his own, and that it was therefore no inconvenience to have the man stop in on my mother as well. I was very little at the time, but I retain memories of a plague of relatives and the calm, slight figure of the physician bending to murmur something to my father. The physician could not save her. I remember the day she died, I think, and my uncle taking me out of the house for a walk. The big red-faced man was unusually subdued, and when we got back, my father kept embracing me, and I was frightened. I remember various maiden aunts and a weeping housekeeper, but oddly enough I remember my mother not at all. She has remained a white vacancy to me all my life. Like my uncle, my father never remarried.

2

Jib Grasshorn

Polly did not stay angry at me, and I was incapable of staying angry at her. She ruled all my thoughts, and the war rattled on without me.

But now, having made so much of my youthful stupidity, I am forced to confess that it had its limits. I was not quite so piggishly ignorant of the events about me during those epochal days as I have indicated, though the quality of their impression on me has been obscured, partly by time, and partly by the popular legends that have been dinned into me.

However, I well remember my father coming into the shop one day gravely disturbed by a pamphlet whose authorship was the best-shared secret in Philadelphia. It was *Common Sense* by the Englishman Thomas Paine, and my father was unhappy not only because it swatted at all our assumptions about the existing government, but because it spoke of certain rights of man which he saw as leading directly to the confiscation of his watches and clocks. But my father was not a foolish or an ignorant man, and he knew that this little book was going to reverberate. "This man Paine has been in our city less than a year," he grumbled, "and already he's stirring up a hellish row."

He handed me the book, all soggy from the wretched January weather, spoke of the consequences of "an inflamed mind," and left me to read it, which I did. God knows, it did not make me rush for a musket, but it was considerable of a tract. We had been engaged in some kind of a war for months, but early in 1776 nobody really knew what we hoped to accomplish. The soldiers were striking back at specific grievances. There had been real battles, and a campaign was underway, but it was momentum rather than any clear goal that carried the war along. The outcome generally desired was one that would make everything the way it had been in some happy time before the last war. Nobody knew quite what might bring this about, but I had never heard anybody speak for independence. However annoying England's parliament and king might be, they still represented the best government in the world, and that was that. Some blood would be spilled setting things aright, but once these differences were resolved, we would be Englishmen still, none the worse for our family quarrel. There was, of course, a certain nearsightedness about this view, since every day brought more misery, resentment, and chaos upon us; but never mind, soon they would listen overseas and all would be well. So we thought, while General Gage lost a thousand men on Bunker Hill and an expedition moved toward Quebec and the guns of our new General Washington pecked away at Boston. So we thought, while tarrings, featherings, burnings, and atrocious castrations were practiced by Tories on rebels, and by rebels on Tories. So we thought, while trade disintegrated and prosperity languished and we learned that our homeland was recruiting German lackeys to send against us. So we thought, really, because we had no other thought.

Paine's pamphlet gave us the other thought. Lightly instructed as I then was, while I leafed through it, smearing the pages with watch oil from my hands, I began to see why it had so disturbed my father. Here was an eloquent damnation of hereditary monarchy and the bald assertion that while our government was better than that of the Turks, it was nonetheless a poor thing compared to what we could have. There were ringing passages that thrilled me even before I could get the sense of them. And, finally, there were soundly reasoned arguments about the wonderful prosperity and free trade with all the world that was sure to come in on the heels of independence.

I liked the bravery of the discourse and told my father so. He shook his head sadly and said that it was nothing but ideas, fragile, untried ideas, and if liberty as Paine saw it was so salutory a thing, why had it never been practiced? I said something about the Greeks, but he would have none of it. "Yes," he said, "that's it; that's all of it. The Greek republic, and where is it now? It did not last, and that should indicate the folly of independence." Such was my father's idea of learning from the ancients.

On my part, I was happy that I'd gone through the pamphlet, because in the next month everybody read it and talked of little else.

In fact, that very evening, while I was tidying up the shop, Jib Grasshorn ran in clutching the booklet and breathing fire. Jib, my closest friend, was learning from his father how to turn a dollar in the ship chandler's trade. He was lively, noisy, high-spirited, and excitable, and the business of supplying gear for voyages on which he could not go bored and irritated him. He spoke a bold game but was considerably less reckless than he liked to appear. He made much, for instance, of the gamy diversions of Hell Town down on the riverfront, but I suspect that fear of the pox kept him from spending much time there. He was bluff, a good companion, and good-natured enough to laugh occasionally at his own braggadocio. He was also a wonderful gauge of the existing mood, so when he appeared with the book, I knew that my father had been right about its import.

"Here it is," he called, brandishing it. "Ah, Freelon, the word we've been awaiting!"

"*Common Sense?*" I asked loftily. "Oh, yes. I read it earlier today. Parts of it are quite good."

This nettled him, and he shrugged off his coat amid expostulations: "Quite good! Ha, it's the triumph of the age!" He glanced around at the watches and

20

snorted, "Look! Look! You spend your youth with these fussy little things and still feel free to offer this book such small praise?" He riffled through the book and boomed out a passage that called King George a pharoah or a toad. "See, there's the truth of it. That glutted oaf bleeding our country. Ours, not his, Freelon. It's just as I've said."

"The last thing you said was what everybody else was saying, that the king was a well-intentioned man deluded by bad advisors."

"Don't be snotty, Freelon. This is a titanic thing — listen . . ." And he declaimed some sonorous, splendid passage until my father came into the shop and regarded him sadly.

"Oh, this is a small surprise," he said to Jib, "that you should be the first to be swayed by this shrill, incendiary essay."

"If that is so, then it prides me, sir," said Jib grandly, but he set the book aside.

"Well, Jib, don't let it inspire you into the grave."

Jib said that it seemed a cause well worth dying for, and my father replied, "You will better be able to judge that when you are my age," and went upstairs, leaving Jib standing foursquare and determined in the glory of his young manhood.

I finished tidying up the shop while Jib relaxed into a series of complaints about the life of a fledgling ship chandler. At one point I interrupted him to ask whether the pamphlet was, in fact, likely to send him running off to join Washington, as he had intimated to my father. He said that he would join up "in due course" and then, grinning, allowed that for all the tedium of hemp and cordage, it did not bring one very close to grapeshot. I agreed and then bundled myself up to set out for a ritual evening of trying to edge closer to Polly by subjecting myself to endless conversations with her baffling collection of aunts and cousins and her solemn father. Trudging toward her home through the wicked January wind, I wondered to myself if grapeshot could be much worse than the ordeal that awaited me.

The evening passed as I had expected, with me sitting in the Lycott's well-appointed drawing room in great discomfort while the aunts exchanged a lot of argle-bargle about the events of the day. At one point somebody mentioned "that dreadful book," and Mr. Lycott made one of his infrequent contributions to the conversation by saying, *"Common Sense* indeed. Surely you are not anxious to discuss this book, are you, Freelon?"

I quickly replied, "Certainly not, sir," which was true enough. Polly smiled at me in acknowledgment of my tact, and I returned to nodding at cheerful banalities. So ended my devotion to the principles of *Common Sense*.

Jib's excitement, it seemed, declined just as quickly. He was still around to grin and chatter with me when, after a bleak season of winds, February turned into March and, amid gusts of gray rain, spring began to soften the ground. It seemed to me to be the threshold of a most promising time; I hoped that Polly would thaw toward me in the sympathetic weather, and Jib was full of plans for half-a-dozen young women. He spilled constant boasts about them, but I am sure that most remained ignorant of his existence. Jib had an odd way with women; he would by fits and starts be stricken with a terrible shyness which stunned him into silence for long periods. Then, when he finally found his voice, he would burst out with something either incoherent or inappropriate. I remember one such incident that spring when we were stolling through the city with a pleasant girl named Margaret. Jib had confided to me that she filled him with the most tender feelings but that when he was with her, words turned to sand in his mouth. So as we walked, Jib was silent as the tomb, glumly shuffling along like a plowboy, while I distracted her with God only knows what silly stories and observations. At length I ran dry and made an effort to draw Jib into my soliloquy. "Well, Jib, you're awfully quiet. Don't you have anything to contribute to my wisdom?" Jib, with luckless inspiration, pointed to where two dogs were mating noisily nearby and gave Margaret a frightful burlesque wink, alarming the girl considerably and wrecking his chances with her forever.

General George Washington was having better luck with his endeavors than Jib; the cause that I had no right whatever to call my own was prospering. The day after the incident of the mating dogs, we got word of the evacuation of Boston. This time Jib heard of events before I did, and sought me out in the store. He explained, with great exultation, that guns driven overland from Ticonderoga had weighted the balance sufficiently to force Howe to pull his troops out of the city and sail away. "It's good work, Freelon — there's not a British soldier in the colonies now. We've won the war, on the face of it. I really ought to get into it before they go off for good. Perhaps they already have."

"Oh," I said, "they'll likely be back."

"Well, then, we'll drive them again."

I nodded and looked concerned but could not truly imagine an outcome that would effect me one way or the other. I did like to think, though, that I was living in interesting times. Jib and I drifted into a rather idle argument about what would happen and what we ought to do. We discussed the war now and again thereafter, but most of our talk revolved around Jib's pointing out the dogs to Margaret. That afternoon's work was much more than a mere gaffe to him, and we had long, weary conversations about what had inspired the outburst.

I rather liked helping Jib bemoan his lot since I was so pleased with my own. But my friendly concern for Jib evaporated in a moment when a dreadful thing happened.

I was chatting with Polly in her home one rainy April day, doing my best to convince her that the life of a Philadelphia watchmaker was one long feast of delights, when she interrupted me by placing a hand on my sleeve.

"Freelon," she said, her face all pinched with worry, "I so enjoy seeing you, but Sligo feels we are together too often."

"Does he, by God?" I said, greatly startled.

"Yes, he does. And," she went on, with a horrible

24

sweet expression on her face, "I do not feel right in distressing him. He is so kind to me, and so intelligent, and so attentive to the desires of his parents . . ."

I do not recall the rest of this revolting discourse, for I was barely listening. I had, in uncertain moments, worried that Consett might be getting the edge on me with Polly, but I had never really believed such a thing possible. And now here I sat, being told by Polly herself that I should stand aside for a rival I had thought beneath my notice. I got to my feet, very sick at my stomach, while Polly was saying how much I would like Sligo if only I took the trouble to make friends with him. I said that a girl who preferred a stick like Consett to me was a girl well lost, and stormed out of the house. On my way through the hall I stepped on a sleeping cat, which fled screaming.

I had no sooner reached the street than whom should I meet but Consett, coming to visit his beloved.

"Freelon," he said, holding out his hand to me and showing all his long, horsy teeth in what he thought was a smile. "I hope — "

He never got to express his hope, for I gave him a sharp push in the chest as I went by, tumbling him over backwards into muddy water and horse droppings. I had one satisfactory glimpse of his long arms and legs waving; then despair flew down on me, and I walked the streets aimlessly in the rain, close to tears.

I thought of seeking out Jib, but I knew what he could offer me — elephantine tact interrupted by bursts of comradely derision — and I wanted none of it. While spring turned to summer and Washington

25

brought his army down to New York, I shunned Jib's company. I was in pain, and my occasional bouts of swinish drunkenness did little to help, though they did bring on some lively instruction from my father. I insulted everyone I knew, kept to myself, and was generally disagreeable.

This evil-natured thrall was broken by an interesting event, which had even larger consequences than to snap my mood and reunite me with Jib and companionship in general.

We make much of the Fourth of July now, but the day I remember was a Monday, the eighth. I was up early with a bad taste in my mouth and a sour disposition to keep it company. I opened up the shop, fussing and muttering to myself about the day. I have never been partial to Mondays, however dreary the Sunday that precedes them, and today I had three dials to re-silver. It was a still, clear morning, with a certain amount of freshness left in the young sky which would burn away by nine o'clock. By ten my clothes would be sopping and I would be nauseated from my task. Still, I began to feel calmer and unable, despite my efforts, to hold on to my resentments. My father was moving peacefully around upstairs with his little domestic bumpings, and I was setting out the watches in a nice order of my own choosing.

I was surprised to hear off to the north of the city a churchbell. I thought at first that some poor people had a fire to contend with. But then another bell started, very close by, and another and another until the morning was filled with their cool justling. And here came

26

Jib, up and dressed and happy, proclaiming that I had better leave the watches and come to the State House. "There's a proclamation to be read, something important." Then I remembered that this was an election day, and said so, but Jib dismissed that with a shake of his head. "No, no. This is no mere election day. Come along."

I insisted that I couldn't; but now all the bells in the city were clanging, and people were starting to move down the street in one direction. My father appeared in the shop, nodded politely to Jib, and astonished me by suggesting that I leave my duties for a bit to see what was happening. So I joined Jib, feeling a little guilty and quite excited. We walked to the State House yard, where a circular platform had been knocked together. A few people were milling about on the platform, and many more in the yard. I said something priggish about gatherings like this one being an enticement to pickpockets, and Jib made a face and told me to hold on to my piece of the true cross.

There was an odd lot of people in the yard around the platform. A group of sailors were cursing and chuckling behind us, and shopkeepers fingered their leather aprons and spat contemplatively onto the ground. Draymen wandered in from Chestnut Street to elbow their way through a little group of noisy, pimply apprentices. A crazy old Negro wandered by, pointing alternately to his feet and to the sky. Two men from the country, very dirty and wearing greasy buckskins, stood together with the unremarkable patience of trees. A drunken man took down his breeches and was hustled away by his friends. Near me, a beautiful old man in a gleaming black coat leaned on his cane, smiling as though God had just complimented him on his clothing.

Men began to leave the platform, until there were very few left. I recognized Benjamin Franklin sitting there and noticed a negligent young man who kept shifting his long legs; Jib told me that he was Thomas Jefferson. (I had seen him a few weeks before when I paid a shilling to view a monkey. The only other man in the stuffy little museum at the time I entered was, I now realized, Thomas Jefferson. He was peering at the small, alarming creature as though it were the sole reason for his visit to Philadelphia.) Someone behind me said that John Hancock, who was from Massachusetts and quite wealthy, was there, too. There were several others, of course, but I did not recognize them.

Toward noon the crowd settled down and a man came to the front of the platform and began to read from a sheet of paper in a fine big voice. So there I heard the Declaration of Independence — you have all read it since — in the stifling noon of Philadelphia summer, with the churchbells still going in the distance.

After it was over, and we had become the United States of America, I waited for the cheering to start. For an instant there was just a murmur of voices, and I heard somebody behind me say, "Now we're going to have to help out those New Jersey bastards." But many in the crowd urgently desired independence from Britain, and soon they were all yelling, and Jib and I were yelling with them.

People began to disperse to taverns and bonfires. I had no thought of going back to the shop that day, and Jib and I were deciding where to begin our celebrations when I heard my name being called and turned to see my uncle working his way toward us.

"Halloo! My devoted nephew and his friend Jib Grasshorn. Storm clouds always gather thickest round your heads, eh, you fine young bravos? Good, good, here we all are, met in the city of Philadelphia, brightest star in the diadem of cities that enoble our new republic." He clapped me heartily on the shoulder and bowed briefly toward Jib. My uncle delighted Jib, and this mock effusiveness set him fairly dancing. "Quite a day, quite a reading; come, you brave republicans, and we'll lift a horn to the fortunes of our new nation." Talking all the while, he bounced us across Chestnut Street through the crowds and into a tavern. We seated ourselves about a table, and he called for brandy. I knew at once that he had already taken some, but now that we were seated, I was surprised to see that his eyes were bleak and shrewd, belying the smile that hung on his broad red face.

"Well, well," he said, when the brandy arrived, "it's a fine season for heroes, lads. Here's to the United States of America; confusion to her foes, and prosperity to her friends, wherever they may be." Some people at a table nearby overheard this and cheered, and my uncle turned to include them in his toast. When Jib and I had finished our brandy, my uncle pressed more on us, and then more still. I began to get the familiar feeling that the people around us were all excellent fellows.

Coupled with this there came a sweet, half-sad presentiment of great events taking shape. My uncle seemed the most affable of men, and Jib the best of comrades. Spokes of dusty afternoon sunshine came in through the windows and lay warm across our table; it was a fine thing to be drinking with companions at this unlikely hour.

My uncle had been chattering with Jib, but now he addressed both of us in what was, for him, a low voice. "Well, my bantams, will these celebrations carry you into the line?" Jib and I looked at each other and then back at him, and, on impulse, nodded. Jib always liked to swagger, and I, smarting still from Polly, felt the old urge to go for a soldier.

The smile fell from my uncle's face, leaving it solemn as his eyes. "Then mind me now, for I will say this to you but once. I know how you feel, for I felt as you did on a time. Oh, you think a little war becomes a young man, and that it will be all marching and charging, and then when you come home blooded, the girls will squeak and squeal and climb on you. Well, I went up to the Lakes — as, you'll say, I never tire of telling — and it's a filthy thing even before the business of killing. Your bowels get out of order, and you walk more than you ever thought you could while you're leaking from every opening, and then you sleep on the ground and some smart whoreson tells you to get up and walk some more. So you do, and at the end of the walking you get more scared than you ever thought you could be. After the fighting, you don't love yourself, because you recall that you thanked God that your friend's brains got spilled instead of your own. Then you go home to find that everybody has done well while you were away, and nobody is interested in hearing about your adventures."

He had turned his attention entirely away from Jib now and was holding my wrist. "I play the fool, Free-lon, because it gives me privacy, and because I have a taste for it. But I will not be fool enough to send you off to the war with a smile and a stirrup-cup. Stay here, learn about watches, marry somebody, have children. Do what your father wants you to do." The transition from genial host to grim advisor was so sudden and complete that even Jib had been struck grave by it.

"But sir," he said, "surely it is nearly done with. The army has gone, and we have made our minds known. I think — "

My uncle swung toward Jib and interrupted him. "Nearly over is it? Because Howe was cheated out of Boston? Because of good luck and winter? What do you think that fleet off New York is about? Do you think they have sent ships of the line to say hello and engage in trade negotiations? Is this wonderful display of England's navy a greeting or a plea? They're here to kill Americans, boy, and if you swagger up there, they'll sure kill you as well. And they can, sprout; they can. Where is our cavalry? Where are our regulars? Where is a general that did anything but put on a uniform and surrender a fort? I am not prepared to judge the philosophics of the situation, but I know who can win a war, and I know what happens in the winning.

"Now" — and, in the smallest pulse of time, he was my uncle again, all salacious good nature — "I'm dry from all this talk and you must be as well, so here's refreshment, and good health to you." Jib grinned, and my uncle treated him to a tale about a slut in a tavern in Hell Town who could take a coin off the table without using her hands. He sent Madeira to the table that had cheered us earlier. Then, with much leering and posturing, he made his farewell.

Jib and I followed him out of the tavern, not wishing to pay for more spirits which we hardly needed. We made our way over to the commons, where militia were firing a volley, having just heard a second reading of the Declaration. I had been disturbed by seeing that unlikely facet of my uncle, but out in open air the feeling disappeared. Jib and I walked up one of the city's excellent broad streets, joined a crowd who were feeding the weathered sign of the King's Arms Tavern into a bonfire, and then passed on to another bonfire. There were bonfires all over the city that afternoon, and the bells kept throwing their silver down on us. It was not long before we decided that it might be wise to invest our own money in brandy after all. We did, and did again. The day lurched toward night, and every now and then I noticed the softening of the light and was quietly pleased with my powers of observation.

When darkness fell, it looked as if the city were afire from north to south. Some of it was, for we saw a few diligent citizens trotting past us with a hose wagon. I had an impulse to follow them, but Jib told me that there was better service for us to perform. So finally I found myself standing in a line amid a crowd of people who were shouting and offering me flasks. After a happy spell I came to a plank stretched across two barrels with smiling men behind it brandishing papers and inkwells. Everyone was uncommon friendly and meant me the best, and I resolved to do the best I could for all of them. I said something about "damned fat King George," which was much more respectfully treated than when I'd tried it on Polly. Jib was beside me, pointing to his signature on a sheet of paper, and a handsome man in uniform referred to me as his brave friend.

When I awoke in the first wash of daylight the next morning, sick and shaking and scared of death, I was a soldier.

3

Captain Totten

I was not immediately aware of my new situation. I remembered a great deal of running back and forth through the city, the fireworks lifting and dropping all night long, and a number of taverns where I drank too much and was inordinately fond of Jib. I felt hellish. I lay on my bed, besieged with formless worries, irritated by the perfect day that seemed to be gathering itself outside my window. I knew it was early because my father was not yet up making noise. In fact, I was drowsing and moaning enwrapped in perfect silence. I could hear the house in its small shiftings. What I wanted most was water, but the efforts necessary to get to it far outweighed my desire. I was teasing myself with my dryness when I remembered the torches, the line, the damnable barrels with their slab of wood and the documents, and I remembered affixing my name there while people I would never see again in my life cheered and nuzzled me with friendly fists. I pushed my face into the bed, but that climactic scene floated brightly in my mind. Finally, with all thought of sleep vanished, I pushed myself out of bed to plod around the room, pulling on dismal scraps of clothing. I peered out into the street to reassure myself with the expected vista and, not the least reassured, made my way downstairs.

My father was, in fact, awake and in the shop working with great concentration on a watch. I shuffled into the sunny room, which was all asparkle with gold casings. My father turned toward me.

"Good morning, Freelon. I waited as long as I could for a report of the doings at the State House, but at last I had to sleep. So it's to be independence for a month, and then ruin on all of us. How did you spend the day?"

"I was at the State House," I said with fragile earnestness, "and I heard it read, and then Uncle Jonas took us for some brandy and we talked . . ." Then the awful bleakness of my situation overcame me. I turned straight to him and cried, "Oh, father, I'm to be a soldier."

He gaped at me and lowered the watch to the table with a thump. I stumbled through the tale as best I could under his shocked gaze. I was too weak to tell anything but the true reasons for my appalling action, and as I talked, he began to shake his head very slowly from side to side, never taking his eyes off me. When I was through, he said nothing and I looked around the shop, which this morning seemed inexpressibly dear to me. My attention was brought back to my father by no word of his, but by a sharp and final sound that alarmed and perplexed me. He had taken the watch on which he had been working and hurled it to the floor. The cogs and springs were even now rollicking about the shop. It was the most impulsive thing I had ever seen him do, and I very nearly wept.

"God damn you for an imbecile, Freelon," he said, not loudly, but hard enough. "You have chosen to take part in a contest that has nothing to do with you, and you have chosen the losing side. The losing side in a civil war. Even if you survive the war, you won't survive the peace. This is a criminal thing, Freelon, and the participants will be punished. God Jesus, do you think I enjoyed losing my wife so much that I want to lose my son now, too?" Then, with the parts of the broken watch around his shoes, he bent his head down and sobbed. That was too much for me, and I wept, too. We stood there choking and sniffling while the morning wagons trundled by on the street.

This fine military vignette was interrupted by Jib, who came into the shop wearing as hangdog an expression as ever I've seen on a human being. He had obviously not gone home but had slept somewhere in his clothes, which were clotted with dirt and damp with dew. "Good morning, sir. Good morning, Freelon," he said, and shuffled over to a chair, greatly wanting to sit down, but conspicuously ill at ease.

"Sit down, Jib," said my father, who had recovered

36

his composure. I danced foolishly over to the chair, hoping that this hostly activity would draw Jib's attention from my face. He seemed, however, not to notice much at all as he sank down and clasped his hands together between his knees.

We all peered back and forth at each other in a tight silence until Jib, in a clumsy attempt to lighten the situation, pointed to the ruined watch. "Oh, Freelon," he said. "Did you smash that?"

"No," said my father, "I did." Which last kept us all quiet again for a little while.

"I did not mean to make light of the damage," Jib said at length.

"It is little damage, considering the rest." My father looked toward Jib and me, who were now posing together, me standing a little behind Jib, my hand on the back of the chair.

Jib was without his usual spirit and bluster. He shrugged and said quietly: "I understand that with this current warfare, much fighting is done from behind things — rocks, trees, fences. That, at least, will be to our advantage. Also, sir, we are signed up for six months only, and much of that will be devoted to training us to be soldiers. We may very well never see action at all."

This happy thought had not occurred to me, but it sounded well reasoned as Jib presented it. How quickly could they see fit to throw us into the field? Not without a good deal of preparation, certainly, and proper equipment. Why, just getting us close to the enemy could take months. And so far, the enemy had done nothing at all save send a fleet. Even now, there might be negotiated a peace which would put a stop to all these proceedings. In my shaken and fuddled state, I had carried downstairs with me the conviction that in signing that paper the night before I had signed away at least a leg, if not my life. But six months was not so long a time, after all, and Washington had a great many soldiers between the British and the precious city of Philadelphia. Why, we might be kept on hand just to defend the city, march around in the afternoons, and be disbanded without once having spent a night out of our own beds. Afterwards, I would have every right to say that I had borne arms in the great civil war.

Jib and I began on the instant to cheer ourselves up with these and similar thoughts, and my father, after a few gloomy head-shakings, proved ready enough to join in. We passed a pleasant half-hour in mutual encouragements.

At length my father asked me who was to command my unit, a question that I could not answer. Jib must have had more of his senses about him than I the evening before, for he said, "A Captain Samuel Totten, who was with Amherst at Louisbourg in the last war."

"Indeed he was, " said my father. "And, as I recall, not a day went by thereafter that he didn't tell some interminable tale or other about his experiences there. He was a friend of your uncle's, but they had a falling out over a woman."

"What sort of a man is he?" asked Jib.

"I only remember that he served at Louisbourg and that he was fat. I should imagine that he is a competent soldier, although I hope that his talents will not be called into play."

I asked Jib whether he knew who else was in with us, but he did not. My father wanted to know when we would start soldiering — another detail that had not interested me when I signed up — and Jib said, "We're to meet tomorrow morning in the yard near Chapp's tannery. We're to supply our own muskets."

This requirement disturbed me, for although, like all young men, I had on occasion fired a musket, I did not own one. I asked my father whether he did and was told, "I do not and never have," as though a watchmaker would be disgraced by owning a firearm.

"Well, here's luck, Freelon," said Jib. "My father owns two, and you are more than welcome to one."

"As well he might be," snapped my father, "since, Jib, I do believe he would not find himself in this situation had it not been for your encouragement."

Jib protested, my father turned to his tools and nodded crossly, and, with the good will of the last half-hour all leaked away, Jib and I left the shop to seek our weapons.

Jib's family lived in a square brick house a half-mile from the chandlery. As we walked toward it, I realized with some surprise that my father had said nothing about my leaving my watchmaking duties. The thought made me feel at once sad and manly. It was a great era for change and ferment, and my father's releasing me from my chores two days in a row without a word impressed this on me more than anything that had gone before.

Jib was still ashen and weak as he shambled along beside me, but he was beginning to be voluble about the virtues of the arms that awaited us at his house: "Oh, they're fine, Freelon. I've fired both many times — this is a rare stroke of good fortune . . ." And so forth until we turned in at his home, went through the front parlor without encountering anybody, up the stairs, and into a large back room that had once housed lodgers during the Grasshorns' less prosperous days. Now it held a clutter of stuff that nobody wanted in any other part of the house. Jib plunged into this haphazard domestic wreckage and took out a bundle of rags tied with rough cord. He unwrapped it, and presented to my view the most beautiful weapon I had ever seen. It was obviously designed for game. The silver inlay on the stock showed a deer coming to grief beneath the hounds, while huntsmen in medieval costume peered out at the real world rather than at their quarry. Jib, beaming, handed it to me, then turned back to the cloths to extract some equipment: a bullet mold, some neatly cast bullets, and a handful of pretty brass things of obscure function. The piece was wondrously light and truly floated in my hands.

"It is most excellent," I said. Jib explained that his father had received it as a gift years before and had never fired it. "Am I to use this?" I asked.

Jib shook his head and led me downstairs again, out through a side door to where a small, neat shed lay flush against the back of the house. He twisted a wooden latch and opened the door on a dark space that seemed to be devoted to the storing of dead things. He leaned into the stale, moldy stench. "It's right in here, Freelon — a fine, serviceable piece. In the hands of a hero such as yourself, it will be the rage and despair of tyrants. Here!" With a great clatter of gardening tools, he pulled forth something that looked to me more like a turnip than a weapon.

The musket must have been almost a century old. It had a great rusted bell of a muzzle and a bore that could have easily accommodated a peach. Its stock dangled impotently from the barrel on a few twists of wire.

"That's very cordial of you, Jib," I said, somewhat amused, but mostly angry. "I'll stand on the field with this, show it to a British regiment and while they're helpless with laughter on the ground, I'll run over and kick them to death."

Jib insisted that the weapon would be fine once it had been polished a little. I complained about it for a while and then thought of my uncle, who, I was sure, would still have his musket from the last war. "I'll take my uncle's musket," I told Jib. "It's not as handsome as your father's piece, but neither does it look like a hoe." I threw the relic into the shed, and we went back in the house, where, on our way toward the front door, we were confronted by Jib's father.

The senior Grasshorn was as different from his son as could be imagined. Where Jib was good-humored, extravagant, and affable, his father was stern, taciturn, and distant. He had the same sense of order my father had, and I would have expected the two men to be friends. My father, however, found the other's company distasteful. He once told me that passing an hour

41

with Hiram Grasshorn was like spending a week in church. This was true, for while Mr. Grasshorn was no more devout than any other successful tradesman, his curt, bleak pronouncements had the forbidding solidity of scripture.

"So, Jib," he said, not favoring me with so much as a glance, "you have come back besotted from a night of whoring and are doubtless taking my hunting piece to pay a gambling debt. Make yourself decent, you rakehell, and get down to the chandlery. Here, put down that musket and explain yourself, sir."

Now we went through the same scene for the second time this morning. Jib told about our joining the militia, and Mr. Grasshorn drew up and in on himself, producing the startling effect of becoming at once larger and more dense. I stuck close to the wall, intending to let Jib face his father without any support from me. The two Grasshorns stared at each other across a silence. Then Mr. Grasshorn shook his head once, muttered something, and pushed past Jib and out into the street, slamming the door behind him. The noise acted as a signal for Mrs. Grasshorn, who darted, blotchy and weeping, into the hall. She was a small, dowdy, defeated-looking woman who had devoted her life to absorbing the iron doctrines of her husband. She threw her arms around Jib and tearfully admonished him to take care of himself, not get killed, and come home safely. Jib assured her that he'd be fine and, in fact, might very well never go away at all. At length he disengaged himself and, with that affectionate mock-reproach that young men use on their mothers, told her to dry her eyes. At last we escaped into the streets, where Jib stood for a moment looking back toward his house with an odd expression on his face. "I'd have been altogether more comfortable with that," he said, "had the old man cuffed me. He thinks I'm going to die."

But the gorgeous weapon was flashing sunlight in his hands, and his abstraction soon passed. We set out for my uncle's rooms, which were three quarters of a mile distant. Jib strode along with the musket slanted over his shoulder in a jaunty manner, happy with the brief glances given him by passers-by.

My uncle received us warmly. He was at a table in his sitting room, noisily consuming a late breakfast. "Hello! Come in and seat yourselves, gentlemen." He gestured toward two chairs with a forkful of husks. "This damnable woman has served me a breakfast that could kill a rat. But your young stomachs can take worse, I'm sure. Let me call for some for you."

We declined, thanking him and explaining that we had already eaten. This was not true, but neither Jib nor I had recovered sufficiently from our night to eat anything.

"Well, I am eating late," said my uncle. "I was spiritually depleted from a long independence night at the gaming tables, and I just now woke up. What is it that has pulled you lads away from watch shop and chandlery?"

As I told him about our errand, he set down his fork and stared at me as though I had turned into a scorpion. Then he began eating again, and when I had finished

43

the now much-told tale, he merely said, "Well, I regret this most deeply. You seem to have spent an even more wanton night than I. I'll not admonish you further; I'm sure you've heard plenty of that from your father. And perhaps there would have been no avoiding this war whatever you did. You are welcome to my musket, of course, and I will fetch it for you." He left the room and reappeared shortly, carrying the firelock. "Here it is. It's not nearly so fine as that majestic piece of yours, Jib, but I'll warrant its being serviceable." He handed it to me. "I remember that it gets heavier with every step you carry it, and you'll need some new flints. It's a chancy weapon and sometimes won't fire when you want it to, but it's the same sort the bloodybacks have. I never did have a bayonet, but here's a bullet mold. I hope good fortune accompanies it and you, nephew; I carried it in the worst fighting there ever was and came away without a scratch." Then, with uncharacteristic impulse, he embraced me. "You're a good lad, Freelon — a little pompous at times and given to shrillness, but those are young men's voices. Be careful, keep your head down, follow your officers, and you'll be fine."

As he saw us out, he asked who was the captain of our company. I told him, and he laughed. "Sam Totten, eh? He's not such a bad fellow, fat old fool though he is. I used to see him frequently, until we had words over some wench. Sam Totten. Well, he's been in it, and he'll be able to look after you. Godspeed, I'll see you soon, and in the meantime I will sleep the better for knowing that you stalwarts are defending my life and property."

Back out in the sunshiny day, we two soldiers marched along the street for a while. At first I found my weapon — which was nearly as tall as I was and weighed a good ten pounds — clumsy and hard to manage. But soon I got it settled over my shoulder in what I thought to be a smart military fashion, and then I felt virile indeed, striding with Jib to defend my infant nation. There were worse things, I figured, than being Freelon Starbird, private soldier in Captain Samuel Totten's Company of Pennsylvania Militia. Our new arms notwithstanding, however, it soon became evident to Jib and me that we had no particular place to go, since the company would not assemble until tomorrow morning. Finally Jib, somewhat crestfallen, said, "I'm getting hungry and I suppose I should put in an appearance at the chandlery. After all, we're not in the field yet." I nodded, but we struck along together a little farther. I hoped more than anything to encounter Polly, but of course such fortunate events never happen, and soon Jib and I parted.

Once I was alone, the firelock seemed conspicuous and showy to me, and I headed back to the shop as quickly as I could. My father was at his post, probing into a carriage clock. The remnants of the smashed watch had disappeared from the floor.

"I've been by to see Uncle Jonas," I said when he gave the musket a melancholy look, "and he very kindly lent me his piece from the last war. The musket Jib offered me was in the last stages of decay." Before my father could make any reply, the door opened to admit Sligo Consett's father. He was a fussy man who treated the world with a sort of arrogant humility, being always your servant, but God's first.

"Good morning, sir," he intoned, "I have a clock here that is in need of your attentions. Good morning, Freelon. I hope that all is well with you."

"Indeed, sir."

He nodded with scant pleasure, then noticed the musket, which I was still holding. "Why, what are you doing with that?"

"I have enlisted in the war against England, sir," I said firmly, for here was one person who was not going to extract mumbled explanations from me.

"Have you now?" he exclaimed, peering beakishly at me and looking solemn as could be. "Oh, I hope this is a foolish jest. A great many hotheaded young men have already marched away from this city, and it will most certainly be their future despair. I am happy to say that my own son has been well instructed in the uses of temperance and will not be a party to this evil. I am not surprised that many young fools might mistake rashness for valor in these unhappy times, but that the son of so respected a citizen as Jonathan Starbird should be one of these fools baffles and distresses me." Indicating that I was no longer worthy of his notice, he turned to my father and said in a most compassionate voice, "I am sorry, Jonathan."

I had been called a fool ever since I had awoken that morning, it seemed to me, and my father had done it in nearly the same terms that Consett employed. However, he seemed displeased to have his sentiments echoed by the man.

"You are quite certain of yourself, sir," he said coldly. "I myself am not so sure that this conflict is solely the exercise of rashness. There have been some formidable minds brought to bear on this issue, and I would find it hard to say that one party has been more guilty than the other in bringing bloodshed about."

"Quite right, quite right," said Consett, hastily backing off from his unexpected bristliness. "We must look not to the blame, but to a quick cessation of these tragic events, lest our peace and commerce become irredeemably corrupted. In any event, here is my clock, which has left off chiming."

"Are you certain," asked my father, "that a man in your situation can afford to leave his clock in the hands of one who has been so unsuccessful in instructing his son in the uses of temperance?"

"I do not know what you mean," said Consett, and he very possibly did not; he was not a quick man, and the conversation had taken its turn rather swiftly.

"I mean that I am not interested in repairing the chime on your clock. Good day, sir."

"I am at a loss . . ." began Consett, but then stopped, not quite sure where he had given — or why he was taking — offense. He nodded once and retreated from the shop.

My father watched him pass in front of our windows and out of sight, and then said: "I did not hate that. He's right, you know, Freelon — you're a damned fool.

47

But your foolishness has at least rid me of one tedious acquaintance. Now go and resilver the dial on Mr. Quire's clock, for he wishes to retrieve it this evening."

I happily did as I was told, and that night my father and I had quite a jolly dinner. The next day I began my military training.

4

Sergeant Kite

It was high summer in Philadelphia, hot and stinking. My clothing would stick to me like a poultice by midmorning, and by late afternoon I was desperate for the slight cooling that would not come for hours. The whole city smelled overripe, but the stench from the tannery was truly beyond comprehension. It permeated the humid air — seemed, in fact, to replace it — with a pukish vapor that stuck to one long after he had quit the neighborhood. There was no getting used to it, either, for the minor changes in the atmosphere that came with each passing hour released everdifferent exhalations of decay. I can still vividly remember sliding my tongue along the back of my teeth and finding them slick with the taste of carrion, as though I had drunk some foul broth.

The stench struck me the moment I first approached the tannery through the yellow air. The yard was mostly bare, exhausted-looking earth, with some bedraggled weeds here and there. On this barren field, some twenty men stood about, leaning on muskets, peering around, and talking. But for the weapons, they might have been any group of artisans and tradesmen met to discuss a piece of news. Most of them looked about my age, but I recognized nobody except Aaron Thane, who kept a livery stable not far from my home. I had started toward him when I heard myself hailed as "You there!" I turned and saw a tall young man approaching me. He was wearing an expensive coat, one shoulder of which was adorned with a brand-new gold epaulet. "I'm Philip Bryce, ensign in this company," he said and democratically extended his hand. I told him my name, and he referred to a sheet of paper he was holding. "Ah, yes, Starboard, good."

"Starbird," I said.

"Of course," he said, smiled at me, and added: "I'm one of your officers; in addition there is, you know, Captain Totten and then Lieutenant Godkin."

"How many in the company, sir?"

"We are thirty-six in all." He looked past me, and I turned to see Jib loping across the field, carrying his lovely weapon. "Jesus, Freelon," he cried, coming to a halt, "did they assemble us here to avoid the expense of feeding us? What a reek! It's enough to make me glad I'm a chandler."

"You're a soldier," said Ensign Bryce, and asked Jib his name. I noticed him casting envious glances at the hunting piece, but he said nothing. After checking Jib against his roll, he nodded and hurried over to where two other men had appeared on the green. Jib and I exchanged complaints about the smell, and then I went over and said good morning to Aaron Thane. He seemed none too happy, and when I asked him when he'd signed up, he snorted: "Signed up, ha! It was done for me, rather. I was levied." He spat on the hot ground.

I was about to admit to him that Jib and I had enlisted while in our cups when there was a commotion at the edge of the yard and a figure worthy of the ancients galloped into view on a fine chestnut mare. It was Captain Samuel Totten, resplendent in the first blue and buff uniform I had ever seen. From epaulet to cuff-buttons he shone like a window full of watches, and his spurs gleamed on boots somehow unsullied by dust. He sat astride his horse as though born in the saddle. My father and uncle had described him as fat, but he looked to me to be massive rather than flabby. His appearance immediately reassured me; here was a man who looked so much like a soldier that he counterbalanced the effect of the motley neophytes who made up his command. He reined in before us, waved his hat, and elicited a murmur of appreciation that was almost a cheer. Ensign Bryce ran forward to confer with him as another figure appeared on horseback. This latest arrival was a slight man with a huge nose that trained itself around impressively with the movements of his head. Except for an epaulet, he wore no uniform, but he trotted right up to the majestic Captain

Totten and saluted smartly, so I assumed he was Lieutenant Godkin. He exchanged a word or two with our
captain and then turned and spoke to Ensign Bryce,
who gave an unintelligible command. At least, it was
unintelligible to me; it was not to a horrible little fist of
a man who broke out of the knot of recruits and started
scampering back and forth pummeling at us. The
small, bulky figure veered about like an enraged beetle,
cursing frightfully in the accent of our enemies. He apparently knew what he was doing, though, for he
quickly got us standing in two ragged lines, one behind
the other, facing our officers.

Captain Totten looked us over for a moment and then
began to speak. His voice astounded me: it was high,
reedy, and beset with a curious whistling sound, as
though somebody with a tiny wind instrument were
making fun of everything he said.

"My friends and fellow countrymen, we are met here
in a great service. It is now my endeavor to make soldiers of you, and so I shall. It is a glorious cause you
are enlisted in, and honor is twice yours since you have
chosen to serve of your will and inclination." Thane,
next to me, made a farting noise with his mouth, but
low enough so that none of the officers heard it.
"There may be difficult days ahead, but we can console
ourselves with the knowledge that, the greater the tra-
vail, the greater the triumph. I am pleased to have you
all in my company."

We shuffled a little and gave out another half-cheer,
and then Lieutenant Godkin surprised us — and, judg-
ing from his expression, Captain Totten as well — by

hoisting his sword from its scabbard and yelling, "I draw this blade with provocation; I will not sheath it without honor." Then he sheathed it and peered around in oblivious satisfaction. Captain Totten scowled and passed on an order, the noisy insect-man leaped into action again, and our training began.

Our first day of drill was like all our other days of drill, and they have run together in my mind into one long awful day where the sun stuck fast at two o'clock and hung in the molten sky. We were always being screamed at — "To the right face! To the left face! Shoulder your firelocks! Advance your arms!" — and we stumbled this way and that, bumping against one another. The stationary sun grew fat above us through the long days, a great bloated thing in a malicious partnership with noise. The noise came from the little man. He was Sergeant Kite, late of His Majesty's 48th of Foot. A full head shorter than I, he nonetheless frightened me half to death at first. He was sallow and his arms were grotesquely long, but he was all fiber, tight-packed like a good joint of meat. When he singled me out to shout at, I found myself in the strange position of cowering while bending down attentively. More than once during those early days of drill, it struck me that if we were up against an army of Sergeant Kites, we were in very bad trouble indeed.

Later on, after his professional disdain began to wear away, he told us something of his history. His father, a London blacksmith, had been gathered to his reward when a horse kicked him to death. So, as a small boy, Sergeant Kite found himself and his two brothers living in some dismal part of the city in the small, cold place that was the best his mother could provide. How she provided even that, Sergeant Kite never revealed, but it is not hard to imagine how an unlettered Shropshire farm girl might have looked after her children when her husband was plucked from her. Kite grew tough and canny, and, not surprisingly, went into the army at an early age. He was a sergeant by the time he was sent to America to fight the French. After Braddock's campaign, where he took a ball in the leg that left him with a strange, sideways limp, he decided that he had no great love for the land that bore him. He deserted, made his way to Philadelphia, apprenticed himself at a forge, and in time picked up his father's interrupted livelihood. He seemed to have no great animosity toward the British, and I never was certain why he had elected to fight his sometime comrades. It is one thing to flee a hard service and make a different life for oneself, but quite another to bear arms against that service. He must have known that it would go hard with him were he captured and identified, but he never spoke to us of the risks he was running.

He was ferocious to us at first. He frightened and confused us and absorbed all our attention. Ensign Bryce, Lieutenant Godkin, and Captain Totten were always there, as well as another sergeant (a tall, gloomy fellow whose name I did not then know), but they all seemed peripheral figures to us. Our days were filled with Sergeant Kite, yelling order after order from His Majesty's 1764 Manual Exercise.

It seemed to Sergeant Kite that we all took an inordi-

54

nate amount of time learning to use our muskets. I was criminally inept with my piece at first, always barking my shins or stubbing my nose with it. On my behalf, I will say that it was a cumbersome weapon, requiring an enormous amount of handling.

"Half-cock your firelocks!" Sergeant Kite would scream at us through the soupy air, and I would pull the hammer halfway back, to where it locked itself. "Handle your cartridge!" Here I would snap a paper cartridge filled with gunpowder and a ball out of my cartridge box and bite the end off it. More often than not, at first, it would bound from my fingers onto our seedy parade ground, or, if I succeeded in carrying it to my mouth, I would bite it too sharply and spill all the powder. "Prime!" Now, if the cartridge had survived my attentions intact, I would shake a few grains into the priming pan and then, at another order, shut the pan in hopes of preventing the priming from escaping. "Charge with cartridge!" The cartridge with the ball and the remaining powder was now placed in the barrel. "Draw your ramrod! Run down your cartridge!"

Up until this point, I did no worse than my fellows in the drill. We were always fumbling the cartridges or knocking each other with our pieces. But nobody seemed to have remarkable difficulties with this last order, and with some reason. All that was required was that we draw the ramrod from its snug place in the stock and push the cartridge and ball down the barrel with it. Anybody with the wit to place his thumb in his mouth should have been able to effect this simple action, and almost everyone was. But not Private Starbird. The difficulty started on the first day of drill, when everybody was dropping his weapon, choking on the powder, getting the ramrod caught in a sleeve. We were not much that day. Sergeant Kite danced in ecstasies of rage, the veins twitching in his forehead. His abuse was formidable, but undirected until he ordered us to draw our ramrods. I believe that half a dozen of us dropped them, myself included, but it was I whom he singled out. I was stooping to retrieve the slender piece of metal when his great heavy shoe came down on my hand. I made a cat noise and jumped up straight, leaving the ramrod where it lay. Sergeant Kite raised himself on his toes and pushed his face into mine. He was so unexpectedly close that it put me into something of a thrall. He opened his mouth to shout, and I peered dumbly at his teeth, all small and yellow and bright with spittle. But he did not shout. He shut his mouth down, went back on his heels, turned his back on me, and walked off a couple of paces. Then he spun about quickly and said in a conversational tone, "What do you call yourself?"

"I beg your pardon?"

"Your name, boy. I regret not making myself clear."

"Starbird."

He showed his teeth. "Are you making sport of me?"

"My name is Freelon Starbird."

"Oh," he said, still fairly quiet, "I see. That's your name. Your father and mother decided that, if a lad was lucky enough to be born a Starbird, they might as well favor him with a fine Christian name like Freelon.

I suppose it's a whisker better than Offal Starbird, or Dungheap Starbird."

My comrades in arms cheered me by guffawing, every one.

"I have no complaint with my name," I said.

"No, Private Freelon Starbird, and no more have I. A man has no say in what he is named."

I was angry and humiliated, as, I imagine, I was meant to be. He seemed to be scorning my father, whom I held in some regard, and my mother, whom, in the absence of memory, I blindly revered. So I said something silly about one liking to know one's father's name whatever it might be, and could he truly say that *he* did? It was a feeble enough retort, and Sergeant Kite smiled pleasantly throughout it. My fellows, knowing who was going to get the better in this dispute, remained silent, and my words hung in the hot day, fatuous and squeaking.

"I only meant to say," he remarked, smiling knowingly at the man next to me, "that it is a bit hard to lead green men into battle knowing all the time that one of them not only mocks all my efforts with his weapon, but with his name as well. It's no easy thing to be clumsy with a ramrod. A ramrod is light as a feather, and sticking it in your firelock is easy as blinking your eyes."

By now there was a great deal of laughter, immediately followed by absolute silence as Sergeant Kite went into a frenzy. "You're a dunce, Starbird, and you will sure pay for it with your life! You dropped that little ramrod, and you'll be dropped sure! You're a farmer, a

57

bloody little farmer, and your hands will never work!"
He ran at me, grabbed my shoulders, and shook me
back and forth, all the while making groaning noises far
down in his throat. His terrible little mad dog's face was
black-red like old brick and rilling with sweat. His
eyes, cocked a few degrees off mine, were the very dis-
tillate of madness.

"Pick it up!" he screamed. "Pick it up!"

I was God-honest certain that he had never been so
mad before in his life and that he might burst and die
on the instant. When he started screaming at me, I had
been embarrassed, but now I was simply terrified that
he would kill me for my clumsiness. I jumped to
snatch up the ramrod, and, while I was bent down, I
heard from my fellows a curious mixture of exclamation
and mirth that Jib later told me was occasioned by
Kite's spitting thickly and copiously on the back of my
head.

I had the ramrod in my hand and the charge driven
home with a quickness I was never able to exercise later
in battle. As soon as I plunged down the charge,
Sergeant Kite's face cleared and he wandered off to con-
tinue the drill.

He may have dismissed the incident with its passing,
but I never did. In time I got smooth with the rest of
the drill, but always when the order was to run down
the cartridge, my hands would vibrate, tinkling the
ramrod against the muzzle in a manner ridiculous to
behold. But I never dropped it again, and I never again
was subject to the full glare of Sergeant Kite's scorn.

Once the ramrod was safely back in the stock, the exercise went well for me. "Poise your firelocks! Cock your firelocks!" I would pull the musket up and tug the hammer back full. "Present!" Now at last the musket was brought up to the shoulder, where it always seems to be in some fine effortless way in the pictures of warriors.

"Fire!" Here I would pull the trigger, and my weapon would roar its defiance at the pawns of tyranny. But not always; sometimes the priming would whisper away and flint would strike iron to no effect. If the priming remained, then the touchhole could be fouled and the priming would fizz impotently in the pan. But if I had not fumbled and if the contentious piece was in order, there would be a terrifying explosion, the butt would deal my shoulder a vicious kick, and the ball would go spiraling off into the heat devils that danced on the weedy fringe of the field. I always kept my eyes shut tight when I fired, but this, I was assured, made no difference; there was little chance of hitting any target by design. Rather, our musketry was to take effect in the way that our enemy's did, through a random equation of numbers. That is, if a score of muskets spray their bullets in the same direction at the same time, chance dictates that some of the bullets will find their mark willy-nilly. And so it was. We hear a lot about those fabulous long rifles that could geld a gnat a league away, and they played their part, true enough. But most of us went into the field with pieces like men, and it was pieces like mine that pried us loose from Great Britain.

So I began to learn my new skill. Powder and shot

were precious in those days, and we spent little time actually discharging our pieces. Rather, we went through the motions, pulling out invisible cartridges and biting thin air, priming and firing in pantomime. This make-believe added to my initial sense of awkwardness. I felt foolish with a gun, and a perfect dunce when I brought the hammer down on an empty pan. But after a while the sense of silliness wore off, and it was just a tedious, demanding task, which I always performed cloddishly. This, too, changed after a while. One day, a few weeks after we had begun our drill, the musket moved easily in my hands. I manipulated powder and shot nicely, found the cartridges without fumbling, knew where the muzzle of my piece was without looking for it. So did the rest of the company, it seemed, for Sergeant Kite screamed and screamed, but lit on no particular individual.

Through a solid afternoon of order upon order, we went through the cycle of loading and firing, marching back and forth all the while, with nobody dropping his piece or stepping on his neighbor's feet. At the end of it Sergeant Kite said, "Well, you bloody farmers may be able to buy yourselves ten minutes of life in the field after all." Then he turned to Captain Totten, saluted smartly, and strode away.

Before Captain Totten dismissed us that afternoon, he lifted his hat with some solemnity and chirped out "Good lads." Whereupon Lieutenant Godkin shifted his bony frame in his saddle and droned a lot of Latin at us.

Limping out of the yard with Jib, I made the observation that Godkin seemed a fool. Jib, too weary to be jocular, replied, "I don't much want to share his company, but he has been there, and we have not."

"Been where?" I asked. Jib told me what his father had told him. Godkin had been a schoolmaster in some hamlet outside of the city. By all appearances he was a prissy stick of a man. Yet, when the news came in from Massachusetts, he had abandoned his oratory and mathematics and set out at once. His pupils had assembled one morning and found him missing; Godkin was riding north. He took his big nose to Boston, gained his lieutenancy in the field, and, bearing two wounds, marched into the city at the head of a company of men. Then he came home, wanting to serve with his fellow Pennsylvanians. With the exception of Captain Totten and Sergeant Kite, Godkin alone among us had seen action. The weedy little creature was a soldier.

The rest of us were beginning to feel like soldiers, too. With the company moving easily to orders, Sergeant Kite sometimes turned the drill over to our other sergeant, Japhet Clew. Sergeant Clew was a thin, quiet man with eyes as colorless as rainwater and a gray face. He had been a clerk before the war, and, while that did not strike me as a livelihood to rejoice in, Clew's gloomy behavior still seemed extreme. He drifted about the field like a cloud, issuing his orders in a weary monotone. All things to him were dismal, save for Corporal Francis Curran.

Curran was a swart, walleyed Irishman with a foul mind. I found him repugnant and tried to avoid him, with minimal success. As soon as he had learned my name, he would hail me by it two or three times a day and attempt to draw me into conversation with lewd remarks about the marriage act. Not wishing to seem a prig, I would return some smutty nonsense with artificial good cheer, and Curran would laugh in a strange, near-soundless way through clenched teeth. This oft-repeated performance made me dislike both Curran and myself, but, once it had begun, I could think of no way to stop it. Even Jib admitted to being put off by the man. Not Sergeant Clew, though; for reasons I never have been able to fathom, the dismal Clew found in Curran a wellspring of unending delight. All day long the gray man would mope around, looking as if he had near wept his life away, and then Curran would say something about how an innkeeper's promiscuous daughter warmed the bed for the traveller, and Clew would throw back his head and laugh and laugh.

Curran treated everybody in the company to his lubricous interests, with varying degrees of success. Paul Bowen, a sober, well-set-up tinsmith about ten years my senior, had a very beautiful sister. One afternoon, while we were resting on the field and sipping from our canteens, Curran wandered over to Bowen. "I was wondering," he said, "how your handsome sister fares."

"Well enough without you," replied Bowen affably.

"I'm enquiring, you see, because I happen to own something that I'm sure she would enjoy."

Bowen climbed to his feet with no great fuss. "Then keep it in your hand, you filthy Irish pig, and let me not hear you mention my sister again." Then he smacked Curran smartly in the mouth, splitting his lip. Curran lurched away, growling imprecations, and Bowen turned to me, smiling. "There's our first blood spilled, Freelon," he said. "My sister can look after her own virtue well enough, but I so dislike that toad, I could not suffer the opportunity to slip by." Curran stopped a few yards away to scowl and spit on the ground, while Sergeant Clew slapped him on the back in transports of glee, and though Curran had arranged the little pageant solely for Clew's delight.

I looked toward Ensign Bryce and saw that he was amused by these vigorous goings-on, but when he saw that I was glancing his way, he sobered up and turned away. He was an elegant young man who moved with the disquieting grace of a dancing master, and he liked to keep his distance. At first we thought him a fop, but at length it became clear that there was nothing of disdain in his attitude toward us, and so our initial caution never developed into resentment.

Under Bryce's languid gaze, yapped at by Kite, and moaned at by Clew, we drilled and drilled through the suffocating summer. One particular day the sun was so bad that Jib and Aaron Thane both fainted dead away, to the enormous contempt of Sergeant Kite, who appeared on the field the next morning with a shabby parasol, which he offered to Jib.

But, for all the brutal weather, and Sergeant Kite's rage and irony, we were, in the main, content with ourselves. Captain Totten himself had said that the company was shaking down very nicely.

We now had added to our drill the martial cheer of company musicians, a drummer and a fifer. They were gangly boys whose combined ages could not have been much more than mine, but they made a brave noise. Of course, they played "Yankee Doodle" daylong, and I have only to hum a scrap of it now to summon up for myself the whole raggle-taggle pageant: the heat, the stench, the tannery floating like an ungainly ship on its own vapors, the necks of the men in front of me sweated and pink, the warm stock of my musket against my cheek, my flannel tongue in my mouth, Captain Totten's horse worrying the sparse weeds, the trees with their heavy, dusty foilage at the edge of the field, the tepid water we never got enough of, the banging, wheedling music, and all of us stamping back and forth over the baking ground, bawling out that brave and inane song.

Late one afternoon we were interrupted by a raucous shout: "Sam Totten, you horrible fat fraud, what would Jeff Amherst think of your legions?" We all looked around to see my uncle standing under a tree, laughing.

Captain Totten smiled ruefully, dismissed us for the day, and walked over to my uncle. Jib and I followed and stood at a respectful distance while the two men grinned and maligned each other. My uncle gestured me forward.

"You know, you've a nephew of mine in this company."

"Oh, indeed," piped Captain Totten in his squeaky voice, "I have reconciled myself to a life afflicted by Starbirds."

"You're not still blaming me for Meg, you old satyr? Well, she's gone to wrinkles and fat grandchildren now, and it was none of Freelon's affair anyhow. He'll not do too badly, by the look of things, but watch out for him, Sam, for rum will be his undoing. It already has been, in fact . . ."

And, to my considerable discomfort, he went on to tell how I had come to enlist.

Captain Totten smiled at me. "No harm in that — it is how our enemies fill their ranks, and their drunkards make pretty fair soldiers."

"They do, Sam, they do," my uncle said. "I'm happy to see your company parading so smartly, but I fear that these early triumphs of an armed yeomanry may be a will-o'-the-wisp." Totten nodded, and both men stared across the now empty field as though they expected on the moment to see British light horse come charging across it.

We had, you see, begun to get the news from New York. Dame Fortune, who had favored our arms the year before, appeared to have left Boston with the British, and now attended them. All summer we had heard about General Washington's Grand Army fortifying itself in and around New York City. When the great British armada appeared in the approaches to the Hudson River, we rashly ascribed its subsequent inactivity to faint-heartedness. Captain Totten, favoring us with one of his rare jokes, remarked: "They have the ships, full of men as eggs are of meat, but they don't know what to do with 'em, for fear they all may be well cracked." But then the British got out of their ships and, in one day, knocked our army apart. They routed the hapless defenders of Long Island and it was only good luck that enabled Washington to bring his troops off into Manhattan. Now our foes seemed again to have lapsed into inactivity, but we knew what they could do, and there were no more jokes on the subject from Captain Totten.

"Well, Sam," my uncle said, "you seem in any event to be doing well with the boys. I see my nephew hasn't put his eye out."

Captain Totten laughed, "No, he has not. Nor has he dropped his ramrod since Sergeant Kite mauled him for it. This company will do as well as the next in the field."

The four of us started to walk toward home. The heat was more tolerable once we were off the field and under the trees. "It is a strange thing, is it not, Jonas," Captain Totten remarked, "to be training these boys to fight British soldiers. It seems no more than a month ago that we were all of us together fighting the damned French. I remember — "

We were not to hear what he remembered, for my uncle made a rude noise and said, "Come along, Totten, let's hear no more of how you took Louisbourg while Amherst sulked in his tent. I was in that scramble, too, you know, and I cannot say that I retain any warmer memories of my British comrades in arms than I do of the French. From general to private, they thought us hicks. They welcomed us as they would welcome the pox. We ate too many victuals, they said, and shrank from the fighting — now, how often did you hear that about provincial troops?"

"If those are your feelings, Jonas, why not take up

arms against them, now that the time is ripe? There is a need for experienced men."

"Oh, no, Samuel, not I. One war was enough to satisfy my martial appetite. Besides, I gave my musket to Freelon, who has elected to carry on the proud military tradition of the Starbirds."

Captain Totten, who liked no better than anyone else to be drawn into an altercation with my uncle, gave him a thin philosophic smile and said good evening. My uncle announced that he was going to take supper with my father and asked Jib to join us. "No, thank you," said Jib. "These exercises drain all the sap out of me. I'll growl with my folks over a crust of bread and be asleep in my bed before dark."

My uncle was cheery throughout the meal, but my father was disturbed because a shipment of watches was long overdue from England. "It's the war," he grumbled. "*Common Sense*, is it? Common sense to let a feasible mercantile arrangement go to ruin? Common sense to burn cities and spill blood for freedoms we already enjoy . . ." and so forth. The irony he saw implicit in the title of Paine's book had become a permanent fixture in his conversation.

"Now, Jonathan," my uncle said affably, "is it common sense to mope and gloom about something you can't alter? I hear that up in New England they're melting down churchbells for bullets; be grateful nobody has decided to seize your watches for that purpose."

"Oh, they'll be seized soon enough, no doubt. I wouldn't give an acorn for my whole stock when those plundering Hessians get a hold of it." We were all scared of the Hessians at that time, and many who previously had no particular opinion about the war became outraged when it was learned that foreigners had been hired to take part in what ought to have been a family dispute. Here were Englishmen paying German mercenaries to kill other Englishmen. Moreover, the Germans had a fearsome reputation as great, hulking carnivores with black mustaches who never tired of killing, raping, and pillaging. We had been hearing stories of atrocities from New York, about how the hirelings would laugh as they spitted American soldiers to trees with their bayonets. One enterprising local printer had already issued a broadside showing these hellish creatures, all teeth and whiskers and odd-looking headgear, taking their ease on a heap of dead patriots after the action, sucking at long clay pipes.

"Come, come, Jonathan," said my uncle. "The Hessians may still be stopped by Washington; after all, they've not yet had to contend with Freelon. And if they come to Philadelphia, they'll curse at you in German and dance on your watches. In either event, your glooming will not alter the outcome one whit. All that these scowls are accomplishing is to give me dyspepsia. I swear it, Jonathan, your face could sour good wine. Behold your son, equally amused by all manner of vapid things, and learn from his example."

My father allowed that I had little enough to be amused about.

"Well, that's true," said my uncle, all smiles, "for I've

little doubt that he will soon be called upon to forsake the tannery yard for sterner fields."

And he was right. Sometime after the middle of September we got word of a British landing in Manhattan and the consequent rout of our soldiers. Two or three days later we heard that Washington was retreating into Westchester County. A month or so after that, we received orders to join whatever might be left of the 3rd Pennsylvania Battalion.

5

Stench Potter

Now I will tell you what I liked about the great war for our independence, and, although that part of it lasted for less than an hour, while it was happening, I thought it worth a lifetime. The company set out on a jingling fine October morning, in a bright and chilly early hour when the whole city was comfortable with the smell of bread baking. We imagined we made a splendid show, slam-banging up High Street, all in step, with the stinks and shouts of the tannery yard left behind with the summer. We felt like veterans and marched with swagger and spirit. We never had gotten the brown uniforms that were due us — no available material, we were told — but we were all together with our firelocks, and we were soldiers, right enough. In fact, we thought a deal of ourselves that morning. Captain Totten rode ahead, grand on his horse, martial as ever Lysander could have been. Behind him, our infant musicians whanged and tweetled, the noise bringing housewives to their doors. They peered out at us and spread their skirts to keep their children from pushing past into the street. As our small column clattered through the city, tradesmen stopped their chores to watch us go by and give us a cheer. Philadelphians had seen soldiers in plenty by that time, but with the news of Washington's many defeats hard upon them, they were relieved to see we were carrying the war away from the city, rather than waiting to do battle in the streets. So they were willing to spare us a cheer, and if the cheers were a little desperate, we certainly did not notice it.

Jib, next to me, was gaping around in hopes of picking out acquaintances among the spectators, but I, feeling properly military, permitted myself only fleeting sidelong glances. With one such quick peek, I noticed my father and uncle, standing a little apart from a group of people on the corner of Market Street. My father was regarding me with a game smile so unsuccessful that my uncle, who was holding his arm, appeared to be a grave robber supporting a grisly burden. The night before, my father had entered my room, where I lay wakeful with troubling thoughts. He was carrying a candle, and by its light he showed me a large and exquisite gold watch.

"Freelon," he said, "this watch was the most valuable possession of your grandfather. It was once stolen from him, but the thief was apprehended and the watch returned. The thief was to be hanged but instead was pardoned in the general celebrations that followed the great victory at Quebec. Your grandfather was furious about that for the rest of his life." I was trying to determine why he had mentioned this example of my grandfather's merciful instincts when he thrust the watch at me. "Now, Freelon, you are to leave this place and face grave dangers. You know that I still deplore this action, but perhaps you would care to take the watch with you as a sort of talisman." My father was not free with such objects, and for a second or two I was dumbfounded. "Ah," he said, seizing on my momentary silence, "I see you are unwilling to subject so fine a thing to the rigors of campaign. A wise choice, son, and I assure you that the watch will be here waiting for you when you return, as return you shall." He gave me a quick, guilty kiss on my forehead and fled the room. Now, as he stood by my uncle with his death's-head smile, he held the watch aloft for me to see.

My uncle called my name and tossed his hat into the air, cheering and capering with the best of them. My father, for once, seemed unaware of his brother's commotion.

So we left them behind us and swung all the way up High Street to First, where we wheeled to the left, and eventually tramped out on the Frankford Road, where we got lost.

Company spirits had already begun to flag by the time this happened. The day, despite its promising start, had turned unseasonably warm. The fifer had

wilted in the heat, and the drummer was tapping irritat-
ingly away unaccompanied. Aaron Thane, who had
celebrated his departure immoderately the night before,
moaned and curled up by the road soon after we passed
the outskirts of the city. Neither our cajoling nor
Sergeant Kite's worst curses could induce him to stir
another yard. Finally Ensign Bryce scrawled him out a
pass and told him to catch up with us when he recovered. Thane feebly pushed the pass into his coat, and
we left him there. A little later my feet started hurting.
This happened because I had imprudently saved a
brand-new pair of shoes for our departure, and now
they were pinching me. In addition, my new leather
breeches, which I had been advised were proper campaign dress, were stiff and uncomfortable, and tweaked
and nipped at my private parts as I walked. I was ac-
customed to the weight of my musket, but the knapsack
with my effects in it was relatively new to me, and
while it did not in itself weigh much, it seemed through
some alchemy to make my musket heavy as a log. I
was hobbling along like a toad by the time Sergeant
Kite called us to a halt. Captain Totten dismounted
and began to discuss our route with Lieutenant Godkin
and Ensign Bryce. That, at any rate, was what I sur-
mised as I watched, with little interest, the officers re-
ferring to a map and pointing in all directions. Eventually they reached an agreement, and we turned around
and marched back the way we had come.

Toward midafternoon we came upon a farmer driving
toward us with a load of hay. Ensconced in the hay

was Aaron Thane, who jumped down off the wagon as it drew past us. He shouted his thanks to the farmer and turned to us. "Well, boys, what's this? Is the war over?" We were resentful of Thane's day, but not nearly so much as Sergeant Kite, who came running down upon him, screaming, "You horrible little touch-hole! Get into line, you squit! Sleep in the sun all day and then ride back smirky with your pissing wit!" Thane popped into line and stepped along happy as a lark at being recovered and having missed our trip around Robin Hood's barn.

At dusk we came to a large house that we had passed on our way out that morning. The officers went to the door, talked for a moment with the servant who opened it, and then disappeared inside. Sergeant Kite told us to stack our muskets, which we did. Then we settled down to eat our supper. At daybreak we had been paraded past a barrel of bread and told to pick out as many hard, dry firecakes as we could conveniently handle. We were also given some gray salt meat of indeterminate origin. I now found that the bread was hard enough to be useful in sharpening a bayonet, had I possessed one. Jib cracked his open over his knee and then drew back with an exclamation of disgust as a fat white worm fell out. While the outside of the bread was hard, the inside was soft and pulpy, and teeming with maggots. Others had made this discovery and were protesting loudly, to the great satisfaction of Sergeant Kite. "Come along, lads, and eat 'em up" was his counsel. "A little worm never did harm. They're the best meat you'll see this campaign. God provides: first they feed you, and then later you feed them." He put his unwelcome advice into practice by eating a fire-cake with evident relish, worms and all.

This queasy revelation had done for my appetite. I threw my bread away and turned my attention to my feet, which, I discovered, had swollen so much that I could not free them from my shoes. Thoroughly disheartened, I pulled my blanket out of my knapsack and wrapped myself in it. Night had come while I was examining my food, and with the night came a chill wind. I heard some talk about gathering wood for fires, but I was too tired for such a project. While Jib complained about our officers pillowed in goosedown in the big warm house, I fell asleep, sore and shivering. I awoke during the night when a root worked its way through the blanket into my back, and was a long time getting to sleep again. Toward morning it rained a little and got colder.

The rain had its salutory effects, though, for the next day was cooler. The officers came out of the house, all fresh and chatty after a comfortable night. I got to my feet, chafed and aching in every bend of my body. After a breakfast no better — in fact, no different — than our dinner the night before, we set off.

I passed an uncomfortable hour or two, but then I began to feel more limber, and although my feet still burned, I was more comfortable on the march. For one thing, the weather was glorious. God had seen fit to put on display one of those days that make his servants feel the game is worth the candle. Autumn was breathing color into the trees, and the air was quick with the smoke from unseen fires.

That evening, with the sun casting a bloody hue in the thin sky, we stopped by a sagging barn. Near it the blackened bones of a burned farmhouse gave bleak evidence of some political outrage of the past year. This time I had energy enough to help Jib and Shem Bowker, an awkward boy with long girlish hands and a harelip, gather in some wood for a fire. We just had it going nicely when Sergeant Kite came by and told Bowker to go down the road a hundred yards and stand guard. "We're in Jersey now," he said, "and nobody can tell what mischief the mad clodhoppers here might be about."

Bowker loped off, scowling, and Jib made tentative efforts to roast the maggots out of his bread. Finally he fished a piece out of the fire and began to chew upon it dolefully. "It's no good," he said. "They only get warm and go to sleep. Sergeant says you can't even taste them, but I can taste them." I was hungry enough to eat bark, and got down two firecakes before my stomach revolted against the maggots. I was deciding how best to attack my chunk of salt meat when there was a shout and an explosion down the road, followed by a horrible thrashing noise.

Sergeant Kite began to bray and we grabbed for our firelocks. Captain Totten and Ensign Bryce ran out of the barn with drawn swords. I was fumbling a charge, full of bright terrors and visions of Hessian bayonets transfixing me, when Bowker came running into the camp wide-eyed and missing his musket. Out on the road the thrashing stopped and something began to bellow. "What's all this?" demanded Kite, and Bowker began to babble about killing a cow. And sure enough, when we went down the road, there the poor beast was, shot in the gut, lying on its side, and making a fearful row. Where it came from we never found out, but it had wandered up the darkening road and frightened Bowker — who had been defecating in some shrubs — half to death. He had heard shuffling on the road, fired blindly in the direction of the noise, and then fled, holding up his pants as he ran. All of this amused us heartily; even Sergeant Kite laughed and clapped Bowker on the shoulder. "See, man, you've felled an enemy three times the size of any grenadier that ever drew breath. Here, hand me that." He took my musket and put a ball in the animal's brain, bringing its struggles to an abrupt halt. "Poor old cow," he said. "Well, boys, she died in a noble cause. Set to."

So we all had fresh meat that night, which we cooked over our fires on grills made from the flattened hoops of barrels that we'd found in a barn. After the meal I settled back full of good feelings. The sparks from our fires went up through the night, and our stacked muskets glinted in the shifting light. Jedediah Waters, a tinsmith, was so moved by his full belly that he began to sing a mournful air about love lost and broken hearts in so raw and quavering a voice that Jib roused himself from his blanket to throw a stick, thereby putting an end to Waters' brief exhibition.

The next morning we found, to the immense delight

of Corporal Francis Curran, that we would pass through a town called Maidenhead on our day's march. Curran was lively as a tick, treating one and all to predictable jests while Sergeant Clew shook with predictable laughter. An hour or two up the road we came upon a tidy house, whose yard was decorated by a saucy-looking girl with an ample bosom and torrents of rich dark hair. Captain Totten lifted his hat to her and bowed in his saddle with weighty gallantry. She responded with a pretty mock-curtsy, and then Curran called out, "Ho, my dove, how far is it to Maidenhead?"

"Not less than six miles," she replied.

"Then they must be a rare commodity, if it is necessary to go so far to find one!"

"Don't trouble yourself," she called back smartly, "for the supply is not likely to be diminished by your presence."

We all laughed, and Curran, unprepared for this retort, said something about "a fine brace of teats."

"A leering wart like you would do better with a cow." Here the lively dialogue was ended on our side by Sergeant Kite's cuffing Curran's ear, and on hers by the appearance of a forbidding father with an Old Testament beard, who whisked her into the house.

"I'd certainly like to have tarried an hour with her," said Jib.

"You'd probably do better than Curran," I replied, "for you, at least, would be able to say nothing at all, which, in the balance, is better than something offensive."

"Well might you be smug," he said, "after your famous success with Polly Lycott."

We chattered away, never quite annoying one another, until we came to Maidenhead, which much have been a disappointment to Curran, for it was a town like any other. The inhabitants greeted us warmly as we marched through, and some women ran out to offer us wonderful loaves of bread, still warm from the oven. A couple of well-fed men in front of a tavern lifted their cups in "a toast to liberty, and the men who fight for it." Aaron Thane, already developing the cynicism of the old soldier, muttered, "Then why don't you come fight for it yourselves, if you like it so much?" Jib, however, always happy with this sort of attention, waved and smiled as though they were the soldiers, and he the bystander.

Nobody spoke to us at all in the next town we passed through. We were greeted by closed shutters, and one sullen drayman watched glumly as we went by. This taste of the moods and humors of civil war left us a little dispirited.

But the weather remained fine, and we were getting used to the food and the rigors of the daylong marches. I felt well, and when, one evening, we tramped through a little gully soft with drifted leaves and bordered by a copse of trees whose foliage glowed like stained glass in the last of the daylight, I thought I had never been in so beautiful a place.

We kept well to the west of the Hudson River when we got into Northern New Jersey, for our officers had no real idea of where our army might be. The last we had heard, Washington was somewhere in Westchester County, and it was Captain Totten's plan to cross into New York well behind the farthest likely reach of the American lines. Oddly enough, we did not encounter a single American patrol, and the shopkeepers and farmers our officers questioned all professed ignorance as to where we might cross the Hudson in safety.

At last we ventured to a small town on the riverbank, and a handsome big river it was, broad and chilly under the pale blue of the October sky. There was a village on the bank opposite us, which a tavern keeper said was Tarrytown. The man went on to say that he had seen or heard nothing of British troops in the area, and that Tarrytown would be a likely place for us to go, could we but get there. There was no ferry, but a man named Stench Potter kept a fairly large skiff and might be prevailed upon to take us across. We marched down to the river and found Stench Potter sitting in front of his tiny cottage, engaged in tranquil meditation upon a huge pumpkin that rested in his lap. He looked up as Captain Totten trotted over to him. Totten surveyed him grandly from his horse: "Mr. Potter?"

"Aye," he replied in a rusty voice.

"You will take me and my men across the river to Tarrytown."

Potter set down the pumpkin. "Horsepiss, sir," he said. "Horsepiss to you and yours."

Captain Totten drew himself up in the saddle and stared in unhappy wonder at this squat, dirty man who was so addressing him. Jib started to chuckle until

Sergeant Clew turned around and scowled at him.

"You Jersey vermin," said Totten, recovering himself, "I could cut you down for your damned insolence."

"And so you could," said Potter, "but it wouldn't get you to Tarrytown. No, I'll not have some popinjay come up and tell me what I'm going to do." Then he startled us further with an admirable imitation of Totten's piping voice: " 'You will take me and my men across the river.' Now, if you'd fetch up on another tack, we might negotiate a crossing. I could not transport more than six men at a time, and that would mean a number of trips. Hard work, and lots of it. Figure on a shilling a head."

"Outrageous!" squeaked Totten, and he and Lieutenant Godkin began to protest against this robbery. But Potter was not to be swayed, either by Totten's cursing or by Lieutenant Godkin's appeals to his patriotic instincts. Finally, with a show of great disgust, Captain Totten handed the man some silver.

"Thank you, General," said Potter. "Hugh!" A pale young dwarf whom I presumed to be his son came scuttling out of the house, and together they began to pull a canvas covering off a broad-beamed boat that was tied up to a tree at the river's edge. Sergeant Kite ordered six men forward, and they climbed into the boat, Aaron Thane rather foolishly grumbling that he had joined the army, not the navy. Potter and his son jumped nimbly in, each took an oar, and they pulled out strongly into the current.

When the boat returned, six more men boarded her,

81

while Captain Totten pointedly refused so much as a glance in Potter's direction.

Finally there was just one boatload of us left, and I diplomatically held back while Captain Totten entered the skiff. Potter, who had grown quite loquacious, explained to nobody in particular that at sea such honors were reversed, and in fact our senior officer should have entered the boat last. Then, glancing at Captain Totten's bulk, he cheekily remarked that he should have counted him as two men.

"Sir," said Captain Totten, still not looking at him, "will you please get my horse aboard."

Potter guffawed. "Why, yes indeed, General. We'll stow him on the lower gundeck with the other horses."

"I will not leave my horse behind, nor will I pay a penny more to bring him across."

Potter considered this for a moment. "Well, it will be tricky, and I'll not do it with another man in the boat but me and Hugh. But you've been pretty reasonable, and I'll get him across for you."

It was cold and windy out on the river, but Captain Totten's mood had improved with the horse victory. He chatted amiably with Lieutenant Godkin until we reached the Tarrytown landing, where the rest of the company was lying about on the ground, waiting for us.

"Now then," said Potter, "I'll go back and get the horse. It may take some doing, for horses tend to be skittish over water, but don't you worry."

So saying, he rowed back across the river. We watched him climb out, very small in the distance. He seemed to be tying up the boat, and we saw a flash of white, which might have been the canvas going back on. By now Captain Totten had called for a spy glass from Lieutenant Godkin and was straining to see what was happening on the opposite bank. Then he started cursing in a shrill, terrible voice. Stench Potter, it seemed, had mounted the horse and, with an insolent wave, had ridden off into the trees. Totten pulled out his pistol and fired it impotently out over the river, startling some birds and bringing a few soldiers down to see what was going on.

A tall lieutenant in a shabby uniform approached, three or four soldiers at his heels.

"Good day, Captain," he said.

"Good day, and be damned to you," said Captain Totten, very much upset.

Lieutenant Godkin pulled the lieutenant aside and explained what had happened, eliciting a sudden bark of laughter from the stranger.

Captain Totten recovered himself and ordered Ensign Bryce off with three men to find a boat, go back across the river, and retrieve the horse. Then he turned to the lieutenant.

"Excuse me, sir," he said, "but I was momentarily deranged by anger. I am Captain Samuel Totten, with Pennsylvania militia bound for the 3rd Pennsylvania Battalion."

"Lieutenant Clement Brindle, of Colonel Eleazer Brooks' Massachusetts Militia, sir, at your service. I am sorry to hear of the loss of your mount."

Captain Totten scowled and ignored this. "Do you have any ideas of where my battalion is?"

"None in the world, sir. But Washington and the whole army is no more than five miles hence, at the White Plains. No doubt you will find your battalion there. The British are moving, and there will be fighting before long."

"How do we get to the White Plains?"

"Along the Lower Cross Road," he said, and pointed. "Now I must be on my way, sir."

Captain Totten bade him farewell, and we all sat down to chew on our bread and await the return of the horse. As it turned out, however, the horse never did come back. Ensign Bryce managed to get himself across the river, but found no sign of Potter, his son, or the horse. Captain Totten had to be content with a meager revenge: Bryce had ordered Potter's boat destroyed.

It was nearly dark when Ensign Bryce returned from his unsuccessful foray, but the news he brought so displeased Totten that he made us get on the march at once. We blundered along what, in his wisdom, Lieutenant Godkin divined to be the Lower Cross Road and at last, in a dark, leafy place, we were challenged.

The challenger was a New England sergeant, quacking through his nose as New Englanders are wont to do. Lieutenant Godkin identified us, and a scrawny man stepped into the road to examine us by lantern light. "Pretty as can be, all of them," said a voice in the darkness. "Follow 'em boys, and get those shoes when they're shot." This marvelous joke inspired much laughter in the dim reaches off the road. The sergeant gestured us past, saying, "I never have seen any Pennsylvanians lately. Might have all been killed back in Manhattan."

"Run home, more likely," called the jester from his dark perch, and his slight efforts were rewarded with more merriment.

We moved on and after a while came to a clearing where a great many soldiers lay wrapped in their blankets for the night, encamped around a single fieldpiece near a small fire. Captain Totten called us to a halt. When I stood still, I became aware, through my weariness, of a whole army around me in the night. Off in the distance I heard wagons creaking and the rattle of harness. There were orders given and coughs and curses. I saw beyond the campfire another campfire, through whose light passed a boy with a strained face, bent under the burden of a dozen canteens.

Captain Totten talked briefly with an officer, and then we pressed on. We were all nigh exhausted, and Aaron Thane was complaining with every step he took. Jib looked neither left nor right but shuffled forward with his eyes half-closed. I heard Captain Totten say to Lieutenant Godkin, "We have the right army, in any event. Not a uniform to be seen, and nobody knows where anything is. We'll make camp right here and find the 3rd Pennsylvania in the morning."

So we spread ourselves out far enough from a campfire to derive no benefit whatever from its warmth and went to sleep with an army sleeping around us.

6

Sir William Howe

We did not find the 3rd Pennsylvania in the morning because the 3rd Pennsylvania was nowhere near the White Plains. We learned this from a harried colonel whom Captain Totten managed to waylay first thing in the morning. "3rd Pennsylvania?" he said, reigning in his horse and peering down at us. "Why, they're back in Fort Washington. Last ground we're holding on Manhattan Island, and God alone knows why we're holding it at all. We'll be needing them right here before this morning's much older. Don't despair, boys, you'll be able to make yourselves useful." With that encouragement, he galloped off.

We were near White Plains Village, a seedy little town with two churches, two taverns, and a few dwellings, all of which seemed deserted this morning. The weather was, if anything, even finer than it had been for the last few days. The hills around the town were crawling with men, and there was a great bustle about us, for General Howe and his British soldiers were expected to attack on the moment.

This unhappy information was conveyed to me by Jib, who had been told by Sergeant Kite that he would soon be treated to the possibility of a ball through the lungs. I had felt a moment of relief and happiness when the harried colonel said that the 3rd Pennsylvania was not in attendance. If our battalion wasn't here, I reasoned, it wasn't our party, and we should hie our way back to Fort Washington — wherever that might be — and wait on our luck there. But this was not to be. No sooner had the first colonel galloped into the town than another came galloping out toward us, trailing aides behind him. Captain Totten waved him to a halt.

"Captain Samuel Totten, of the Pennsylvania Militia."

"Colonel John Haslet, Delawares. Get out of my road."

He was a knotty, enormously competent-looking Irishman in a faded blue uniform.

"Sir, we were to join the 3rd Pennsylvania Battalion."

"Well, join 'em, God damn it. Did you say the 3rd Pennsylvania?"

"Yes, sir, and since I have been given to understand that I cannot join them, I would like to be of use here."

"Good. There is Chatterton's Hill." He gestured to a long ridge about a half a mile distant. "It commands half our position and there's nothing up there but some militia under Putnam. Take your men up and set 'em down on the right." He looked us over. "They're pretty tidy, Captain. Have they ever been in action before?"

"No, sir, but they are well trained under my direction and eager to strike a blow —"

There was a noise of musketry, quite a ways off, but sufficient to make me shiver. "Oh, hell," said Colonel Haslet, and started toward Chatterton's Hill without looking our way again.

"Men!" shouted Lieutenant Godkin, drawing his sword. "Here is what we have waited upon lo these many months. Now must we quicken to our great task —"

"Get 'em moving, Sergeant," said Captain Totten, and Sergeant Kite, perfectly at home in the confusion, screamed us into line. We started toward a bridge that spanned the small river running along the foot of Chatterton's Hill.

"We're to be soldiers after all," I said to Jib, in what I hoped to be a hearty tone.

He looked at me in surprise and then grinned. "Your mouth is trembling."

The bridge was crowded with soldiers, many of them wearing round black leather hats bearing the legend "Liberty and Independence. Delaware Regiment." A few of the hats were jaunty with red plumes, but the blue uniforms their owners wore were tattered and dirty. The Delawares were making no great fuss and paid us no attention whatever as we got across the bridge between two groups of them.

We walked along behind the crest of the ridge, very quiet. Aaron Thane actually fetched himself up against a root, fell over, and climbed back to his feet without a single complaint. From the other side of the hill we could hear musketry, the irregular popping sounding oddly gay in the pleasant morning.

At last, as we approached the end of the ridge, Sergeant Kite ordered us about to the left, and we began to climb uphill. We went through stands of trees, and fields where the corn still stood ungathered. Before we reached the crest, there came, from the other side, a frightful crashing noise, loud as the Day of Judgment. "Artillery," called Captain Totten. "Never you mind it, boys; it sounds worse than it is."

Putnam's militia apparently thought otherwise, for, on the second discharge, scores of them came running from their posts, over the top of the hill and down toward us. We watched them come, ragged men — this whole army seemed to be ragged — in no uniforms to speak of, running pell-mell, with their officers bellowing and thrashing with the flats of their swords, trying to rally them. Captain Totten called for us to halt, and as we did, a lieutenant with drawn sword grabbed hold of a panicked soldier who stood at least a head taller than him. The lieutenant was just a few yards off from us, and we watched him spin the fleeing soldier around, shouting for him to get back to his lines. The soldier regarded his officer with small, empty eyes for a moment and then, very deliberately, he raised his musket and fired it full into the lieutenant's chest. There was an explosion as the powder in the pan fetched off, but the piece missed fire. The lieutenant immediately produced a pistol and discharged it in his would-be murderer's face. The pistol also fizzed and died, and the two men stood for an instant staring at each other like enchanted beasts as the passion of the moment ebbed. Then the lieutenant raised his sword and in one short, hard movement cut off the soldier's thumb. The man screamed and began windmilling his arms, drawing a circle of blood on the air. Two of his comrades took hold of him as the lieutenant turned and walked back toward the crest of the hill. Some sort of order had been re-established around us, and men were moving reluctantly back uphill to their posts. The artillery had ceased for the moment.

Sergeant Kite called for the company to start forward, and we glumly complied. We were all subdued, but not half so much as when we got to the top of the hill and saw what was on the other side. We were a little while getting there. Captain Totten came up against a great many strange officers who appeared to have no interest in seeing us take our proper place in the line. But finally he asked a timid lieutenant where Putnam's men were, and found that they were all down to our front, so we pushed on and came at last to a captain in Brooks' Massachusetts Militia, who directed us to the right of a scraggly group of men lying along a stone wall barely visible through the trees.

"Sergeant," ordered Captain Totten, "take 'em to the

right of those men." Sergeant Kite pressed us rudely down forward. We came through a final stand of trees, and Shem Bowker, who was filing down ahead of me, whispered, "Merciful God!" I followed him out into the sunlight, and there was the entire British army, pretty as ever pretty could be.

Below us on the plain — which was not white at all, but tawny with dying summer shrubbery — huge blocks of men were wheeling and countermarching in perfect order. Here and there the blocks had spilled off a few men: some to tend more field guns than I had imagined were in the New World, some to dash about with swords, some to ride to and fro with right arms lifted in the bearing of messages. The autumnal sun was now roistering up a clear and happy sky, and its beams flashed off acres of polished metal. Behind the blocks of men, more men were waiting on horseback flickering in the distance. A little in front of those horsemen, mounted officers were conferring, handling papers back and forth, and trading sunflashes that must have been spy glasses for the better study of our sorry position. The music of the regimental bands, whose many instruments I could easily descry, was all about us. Our little musicians were nowhere to be seen, and we had no music at all. As we watched, the enemy blocks stiffened, shifted, and formed into columns. No motions were wasted, save for those of the officers, happily turning this way and that in the certainty of their victory.

"There they are, the cowards," shouted Lieutenant Godkin, and for one terrible second I thought he was going to order us to attack them. "Gird your strength against them, and hurl back their blows."

"Steady, boys, it's not so much as it looks, for I've been with 'em, and they're scared, depend upon it." This was Sergeant Kite, coming down our line, pushing us up against the rough stone wall, settling us down, and slapping our rumps. "They think we're all Red Indians up here," he said, chortling, "and they fear these heights. One volley, and they'll scatter. Oh, they'll make nice marks, too. See how red they are!"

I crouched down behind the stone fence and peered through the coarse rocks, seeing, at my angle, no soldiers at all, but rather lichen and sweet calm sunlight in a narrow tunnel. I would have loved to hold the whole day so, lying on my musket and peering at little crevices, but it was not to be. There was a great noise and a clamoring in the trees above me. I snatched up my head to see all those cannon down below jumping back and spurting out smoke. Tiny men ran forward to charge them as dry branches came scattering down around me.

"I knew this was going to happen," said Aaron Thane, just as the guns spoke again. Jib grabbed my hand and said something to me, but I could not hear him, for all the sunny world had disintegrated into rank noise. I stuck my head back down behind the blessed wall, while the guns banged away and the very air groaned and whimpered with the passage of the shot.

"Here's a laugh, boys," called Captain Totten, and I looked to see him standing up behind the wall, sword in hand, smiling as though at a dance. "They don't have the range, and, damn me, their eyes are so poor they can't get it." But just then a shot smashed into the wall a little ways to my left, and shards of rock came crooning overhead. I saw one of Brooks' men lifted right up into the air, his arms and legs flapping like laundry. He dropped down in a heap, and the men close to him began to creep backwards, always keeping low, until Lieutenant Brindle, whom we had met in Tarrytown, came down the line cuffing them back toward the wall.

Lieutenant Brindle noticed Captain Totten and shouted through the din: "Captain Totten, I see you found the Lower Cross Road!"

Our captain looked at him blankly. "I'm afraid you have me at a disadvantage, sir!"

"Lieutenant Clement Brindle, Brooks' Massachusetts Militia. Did you recover your horse?" Then the lieutenant was gone, knocked down by a cannonball.

"Never mind those pebbles about your ears, men!" yelled Captain Totten, still upright. "They're coming for us now. We can give 'em as good as we get."

I hazarded a peek, and, sure enough, the scarlet columns were moving our way. Jib fired his piece, and Sergeant Kite was immediately upon him: "Hold it in, you baby! Do you think you're here to entertain 'em? Hold your fire 'till I tell you otherwise." Jib rolled on his back to drive home a new charge. "That's right," said Sergeant Kite, now smiling like a father shown the first throbs of his progeny. "Keep low, you beauty. Wait on the main chance, boys. Oh, here they all come. See that fine-looking officer? That's Bloody Bill

Simon, and he was in pickle twenty years ago. He'll fall over if you spit at him."

I looked out over the wall again and saw that, but for the column making toward us, the British soldiers had sat right down in the field to watch the outcome of the contest. This epic complacency touched off the first real fear I had ever known, a cold trickling in my groin that left me too weak to move my firelock. They were the surest soldiers in the world, and if they thought us too poor to waste a whole assault on, then could they be very far wrong? I lay and considered my doom while the great shot clattered through the trees above me.

At last the guns fell silent, and I saw the men in Brooks' command crawling away from the wall, with no plucky lieutenant there anymore to check them. But in a twinkling Lieutenant Godkin was in among them, with none of his rhetoric. "Gaaa! Gaaa!" he shouted, swatting at them with the flat of his sword. They crept back to the wall, but not for long.

Off to our right Hessians came out of the woods. They were every bit as terrible as ever folks back in Philadelphia had thought them to be. Tall as houses they were, with horrible waxed mustaches and long bayonets. They paused to fire a volley, and next to me Shem Bowker went down, shot right through his hare-lip. Never had ball a deadlier direction: he fell and did not move; only his hands trembled a little. Sergeant Kite was calling for us to face around to the right, and we did get off a volley. The Germans, in their huge brass hats, seemed to hesitate, though I saw none of them fall. I rammed home another charge, not dropping my ramrod, and as I did so, I became aware of a scuffling, jingling noise. Beyond the Hessians, cavalry was coming up the hill. I heard the silver braying of trumpets as the horsemen galloped toward us. Captain Totten, behind me, shrieked, "Stand and fight!" again and again.

But it was not our day to stand and fight. The big men were coming on with their bayonets leveled, disdaining any further musketry, the cavalrymen were swinging their swords threateningly above their heads, and it was enough for me. Lieutenant Godkin, at my elbow, said, "Do not disgrace this company!" but I was not stirred by this appeal to our five-minute tradition of excellence in the field of battle. I took to my heels with the rest of the company, and we all fled like pigeons. We got intermixed with the New Englanders and I bumped against a man who smelled like cooking bacon, and fell to the ground. I was up again just as quick as my legs could lift me, running toward White Plains Village, which I thought might offer sanctuary. I fell again, this time over an abandoned firelock, and turned to see how my pursuers were faring. They were very close but were eddying around a single figure. It was Lieutenant Godkin, alone amongst his enemies, slashing and chopping at them. I was not moved to help him in his lonely, gallant task, and, having recovered my footing, kept on with the rest of the company.

We all leapt a wall together and headed for a line of soldiers. I recognized them by their caps; they were the Delawares. There, among them, was Colonel Haslet, who had been responsible for bringing us to this awful place. He had been distracted in the morning, but now he seemed calm, and so did his soldiers. They stood sullen and composed before us, firelocks at the ready, and moved a little to let us get through. One of them actually gave me a yellow grin as I burst by.

I heard them fire their first volley as I came abreast of the three or four men trying to haul off a field gun. "Help us!" they cried, but I kept going. The British column must have got up the hill, for there was heavy firing off to my right and the defenders of the slope were coming over the crest as their lines began to disintegrate. I saw large shapes out of the corner of my eye and realized to my horror that the cavalry was in among us. Still running, I turned to see the dragoons on their mounts sickling down fleeing men. The Delawares were beginning to break, though those nearest Haslet still stood like a rock. When I turned back, it was to be confronted with the frightful apparition of a dragoon directly in my path. He had a tiny red face that appeared to be no bigger than an apple. He sliced his sword down at me, croaking, "Damn you for rebel scum," but a musket went off near us, his horse shied, and I heard the sibilant noise of the sword passing by my ear. I scampered around his horse and did not give him another chance at me.

Though I had been footsore for days, panic gave wings to my feet, and I fairly flew across the smoking field, along with hundreds of other screaming, tumbling men. An officer caught at my sleeve as I ran by, telling me to stand with some men he had rallied. I found myself grinning at the absurdity of the idea, and soon the dragoons were riding down the men who had tarried, more fools they for waiting. I was not going to indulge in pathetic sham heroics while death came at me on horseback.

There was another burst of firing behind me, so someone must have been offering resistance. Good for you and thank you, I thought in odd small lucid thoughts that came and went in time with my breathing, and if ever we meet in the King of Prussia, I will return the favor and stand you a glass.

"You there!" called yet another bold officer. "Get you behind that fence."

"Thank you, thank you," I said, and ran the faster, my mouth dryer than ever it had gotten in the tannery yard.

At last the ground leveled out. I could run no more, and fell on my stomach, gagging at the dust in my throat. There seemed to be no more firing, but it was some time before I could marshal my strength enough to roll over and see what was doing. When finally I was able, I looked toward the heights I had just abandoned so precipitously. There were our conquerors, dressing their lines smartly along the crest of the hill, their trumpets making rich and lovely noises in the distance. They acted completely unperturbed by whatever opposition we had offered them; those straight, fine ranks could have been parading for the pleasure of the king. In bleak comparison, here came the last of our army, retreating sloppily down the slopes, which smoldered fitfully here and there. A few trees showed white splinters where shot had gouged them, but most stood calm in their scarlet and russet glory, and, but for our soldiers coming along like a gaggle of beggars, the hills and plains seemed steeped in peace. The rising columns of smoke might have been part of some harvest ritual.

I helped myself to water from my canteen and immediately vomited it up on my coat. Then I began to tremble. I thought of Shem Bowker's broken face, and of the Massachusetts lieutenant plucked into eternity with such random suddenness. I thought of the grim malice of the horsemen with their long sabers, and I thought of the Hessians with their flawless discipline, and how we churned and blundered to get away from them. Nothing in my training had prepared me to stand against a bayonet charge, and such an ability appeared to me now a dubious virtue. Lieutenant Godkin had gained little enough from the possession of it. The soft afternoon seemed to drip sweetness on me, but had I shambled down that hill into our positions ahead of Shem Bowker instead of behind him, I would be up there yet with a smashed face, all unknowing. I thought of my father with all his small watchmaker's tools, and of the shock and concern he would express were he to know in what fashion I had passed the morning, and I could have wept.

Instead, I got shakily to my feet and set off to find my company. There were soldiers moving all around, heading for the American camp, but nobody I recognized. In my mazy state, I trod on somebody's foot. He cursed at me, and I apologized and saw that he was helping to carry a wounded lieutenant on a litter. The officer had lost his left foot, and the stump of his leg was wrapped in a grimy shirt. He regarded me with bright eyes. "Where were you in the fight?"

"We were next to Brooks."

"Haw. You ran away, all of you. I am with Small-wood's Marylanders, and we could have held 'till Christmas had you not all run out on us. But," he went on happily, "it makes no difference. I've lost my foot, but not my rosy cheeks. Doesn't hurt at all, though I must say I was used to having it there. Well, lackaday, no use weeping over spilt foot. Here, give me some water." I handed him my canteen, but he no more than pecked at it before he passed it back. "Very civil of you, Private. Never in my life have I seen cavalry in action up to this day, and I hope never to again. And do you know what they were tootling on those horns? Fox-hunting calls. Our good General Washington is a fox-hunter." He lowered his voice cautiously to impart this last to me, as though the general might somehow overhear him. Then he smiled broadly. "God damn and blast all Virginians," he said, and his men bore him away.

There were numbers of wounded coming in, most with gray faces and many looking pouty in a strange, childlike way. I pulled my head into my shoulders as some firing broke out to the right, in the American lines that had not been attacked, but it stopped almost at once. I turned to determine the cause of the fire, and in so doing I recognized Aaron Thane, talking to another private a few yards distant. I made my way over to him. He had lost his hat, and his face was very dirty.

"We certainly did run," he was saying with morose satisfaction. "We ran just as fast as we could, every man of us, as soon as they came out of the trees. My, we did run."

His companion, a sardonic, able-looking fellow, replied, "Well, I ran on Long Island, and then I ran again at Kip's Bay, and now I've run today. I may not be much of a soldier, but I am surely turning into a fine runner."

I called Aaron's name, and he looked over and grinned, "Why, Freelon! Still in one piece. We certainly did run."

"We did indeed. Where is the rest of the company?"

"Back in the camp. Come along."

We walked together back of the lines. Everything was in turmoil, as wagons heavy with equipment and wounded trundled about. "They're moving 'em out to the rear, I'm told," said Thane, "to a place called North Castle. Should have been there in the first place, from what I can make out, and we'd never have been dislodged. Look," he pointed, "there's General Washington!"

I looked and saw nothing. "Oh, he just went behind those trees there. Big fellow. Much good his wisdom did us today."

I whooped, for I had just spied Jib, sitting on a broken barrel. He glanced up and beamed. "Ah, Freelon," he said, hurrying over to me, "I thought you were gone. Oh, this is good. Most the whole company came through it." I clapped him on the shoulder and then saw, with some surprise, that he was holding a large box turtle. Its head dangled out of its shell as it regarded this strange, smoky world with polished black eyes. Jib said that he did not know where he had picked it up. "When I got through running, there it was in my hands. But I've lost that beautiful firelock." He set the turtle down. "It seems a poor trade. I must have dropped the piece as soon as we retreated, but I have no idea where. In any event, some damned German has it now, and it's a nice day's work for him."

Captain Totten came over and congratulated me on my escape. He looked as martial as ever, and not a bit disconcerted by what Jib had elegantly termed our "retreat." "We'll hold 'em better the next time," the captain said, "you see if we don't."

I wandered about and ascertained that our two musicians were still with us, though both looked forlorn, and the drummer had startling white tear streaks in the dirt on his face. In fact, all of the company, save for Shem Bowker and Lieutenant Godkin, was present — dirty, torn up a bit, scratched and gouged, but alive.

Nobody professed much of a stomach for food, but when some arrived, we fell upon it like ravening hounds. Sergeant Kite, all approbation, strutted among us as we ate. "That's it, lads, eat up. Nothing like a little fighting to give a man an appetite." I had feared seeing him, but he said nothing about our dismal showing on Chatterton's Hill.

The sun climbed down the sky until the plain beneath the hills was a deep pool of shadow, and still the enemy showed no inclination to press his advantage. As this became more evident, our spirits rose, and when

Isaac Wharton appeared with some more tangible spirits, a barrel of which he had contrived to steal, we took out our cups and got very merry indeed. Just at nightfall, when we were able to see the campfires of our enemy spangling the slopes that he had taken from us, Ensign Bryce began to shout, and we all looked up to see a ghostly figure enter into our midst.

"Good God!" cried Captain Totten. "It's Godkin come back all smoky from hell!" And so it was. He was missing a sleeve from his jacket, and a long, shallow cut in his forehead gleamed wetly in the firelight. He was flesh and blood, though; a little knocked about, but still orating. "In the righteousness of my cause was I protected, and shielded from my foes." This, in essence, was all we could find out about his miraculous salvation; perhaps it was all he knew. He had taken a fair knock on the head and was vague about the afternoon. He had one cup of rum and fell asleep immediately upon quaffing it. I slept soon after, but kept twitching myself awake, every five minutes it seemed, all through the night. The men around me thrashed and moaned, and Jib talked and talked in his sleep, his words loud enough to keep me wakeful, but too soft to be comprehensible. As far as I could tell, Sergeant Kite slept not at all. Every time I glanced his way, he was staring placidly at Chatterton's Hill, watching the hostile campfires.

7

Aaron Thane

I woke from a final curled dream to see a leaf, big as your hat, spiraling down toward my face. Sergeant Kite was shouting, "On your feet, you bloody cows!" and I climbed up into a cold day. The sky was a curious brassy hue around its edges, and a steady wind blew at us. Things had the same color as they did the day before, but winter had walked over us in the night.

Aaron Thane was standing wrapped like a begging crone in his blanket, opening and shutting his mouth in soundless complaint. It was immediately clear to me that the tenuous good spirits that had suffused us the night before had fled with the darkness. I had no sooner gained my feet than I sat flat down again, drained and weak. I was aware of the odors of cooking food, but I had no stomach for it.

"Nice, nice," said Sergeant Kite, addressing the sky. "I hope you brave men have slept well." I rolled on my side, aware that his unwelcome scrutiny had settled on me, and brought my knee up against my firelock, which I lifted with me in a second attempt to gain my feet. As I did so, something rolled out of the lowered muzzle and fell with a tap on the ground. It was a ball; I peered at it where it lay amid the fallen leaves. "Oh, good, save it for breakfast!" shouted Sergeant Kite, snatching my piece from me. "And did it stay the night with friends?" He fished in the muzzle and, to my horror, dislodged three charges — ball, cartridge, and all. "I taught you not to drop your ramrod, Starfart, but not to cherish your shot. Good Jesus, it's a miracle we were able to keep the ground they did not even want. Here, give me that." He took the firelock of George Horlacher, a somnolent baker, and flew into a towering frenzy upon finding in it another unexploded charge.

"Look! Look!" he screamed, gesturing toward Chatterton's Hill with spittle on his chin and his eyes rolling in his head. "There is the enemy, and they are so good with their pieces that they shoot 'em after they charge 'em. If they want to walk across that little field, they will, and cut your guts out, and eat 'em with salt, and wonder when the battle will be!"

His rage had shifted to poor sleepy Horlacher, and I took this opportunity to worm my way behind a tree. I sat with my back to Sergeant Kite and watched my army greeting the rosy dawn. Yesterday, even running away from an army's business with them, these men had seemed dear friends who, but for a rub of the game, would have been the components of a conquering horde. Now they simply seemed absurd. A few yards away, a New Englander interrupted an intense session of nose picking to turn and see why our sergeant was yelling. Tied to his sleeve, presumably for decoration, was a bit of pierced tin that looked like part of a candlestick. He gave me a great wink, which, to my irritation, I immediately returned. I feared that he would take this as a signal that I wished to converse with him, but he did not; he turned away and again went to work on his nose.

Beyond him a fat man was walking in circles proclaiming in the richest terms a great victory the day before. He was small and scruffy and almost perfectly cylindrical, but he had an absurd look of beaming health about him; in his ecstasy he could have been a lump of enthusiastic dough, about to be formed into a soldier. The soldiers near him were of thinner stuff. They sneered and chuckled and picked things out of their clothing, while he ran this way and that preaching at them.

"We did leave the hill, we sure enough did, but only to lure 'em up to it, while we go to stronger ground, where we will draw their claws, and laugh while we do it. Now, my brave friends, I will tell you of a sweet vision that I saw revealed to me on top of a thunderstorm. It has sustained me, and it will sustain you. I had been caught in the fields by the storm and was making my way home when there was a great lightning in the sky. It did not go away but waxed and burned brighter and brighter until I was fair blinded by it. Then the top of the sky rolled down like a scroll, and behind it I saw the most beautiful baby, as beautiful as the Christ child, but in a manger of evergreen and by a wider sea than Galilee. Behind the baby the savages of the forest knelt in solemn wonder, and about the baby great lights ran up the sky. But behind the baby, neighbors, I saw our great General Washington, and in one hand he held a Bible and in the other hand a whetstone, and he was sharpening the Bible on the whetstone, and he was the despair of a bloat king. Oh, my friends, could you have but seen it, you would have stood even as I stood, with the rain shaking down upon me — ”

His heroic vision was here interrupted: the soldier with the tin decoration had crept behind him on hands and knees, and another soldier, equally scruffy, pushed the round little man backwards over the first. The prophet hit the ground with a forlorn squeak of bumped air and lay there for a moment with his arms and legs pumping. Then he bounced up, quick as could be, and regarded his assailants with eyes unclouded by visions. "Well done, neighbors," he said, with an evil smile. "And had you shown such spirit yesterday, on that lost hill, you would not be skulking in the trees down here today." With that he walked briskly away, in search of a better audience.

Behind my tree, Sergeant Kite was still screaming at Horlacher and the wide, silly world. Men were walking around, bumping up against friends and getting in vivid little squabbles, with much gesturing of hands. Many were snatching scraps of food out of black kettles and settling down to chew on them. Everyone who was eating would interrupt each bite with quick, suspicious glances, as though to make sure that nobody was poised nearby to grab the food away.

Jib sought me out and sat down beside me. "I'm weak, Freelon," he said. "It is good for me that I lost my firelock, or Sergeant Kite would have been after me, too. I remember running home my charges, but not firing them. It's an odd thing: we have been well trained in the motions of battle; it should have gone smooth. But everything happened so fast once it started. Give me a minute or two and the tannery yard, and I would have been a hero sure. But this wasn't like anything."

"Well, we are not soldiers," I said, "and there's an end to it."

We all spent the day after the battle nursing sour dispositions, and that night a sparse salting of snow came down upon us. This caused much discomfort to many of the New Englanders around us, whose baggages had been moved back to North Castle with the wounded while they were up on Chatterton's Hill. They returned to find that they had no blankets, and they slept on the leaves with nothing above them save the trees from which the leaves had fallen. In the morning, before they began to stir, the sleeping men with the snow drifted into the creases of their clothing had the aspect of corpses strewn thickly by a catastrophe. Years later I was reminded of the sight when I viewed a painting of the field at Waterloo the night after the battle, with the dead heaped and bunched mile upon mile under the baleful glare of a moon the size of a grapefruit.

I did have a blanket, for which I was grateful. Jib had had the foresight to supply himself with two blankets, but one was stolen off him while he slept. As a consequence, he awoke the next day with a fever — trembling, and hot and cold by turns. The malady would come and go, leaving him weak and lightheaded, but cheerful. When it returned, he would wrap himself in his remaining blanket and sit shivering. For my part, my bowels became griped, making me prey to cramps that near bent me double until I could squat down and squirt out vast amounts of translucent liquid.

I was coming back from one of these painful voidings when I first saw General Washington, riding toward me down the path on which I was returning to the camp. Everyone looks big in the saddle, but he was truly immense, half a head taller than the tallest of the aides who rode behind him. Hitherto, the most impressive martial figure I had seen was our own Captain Totten, but the man before me made a burlesque out of him. The General handled his mount on the narrow path with the negligent grace of the born horseman. He had a long face with a great deal of chin to it, and his eyes were very far apart. If he was troubled by our current situation, his face did not betray it; he appeared neither sad nor happy, nor harshly competent as did Haslet, but rather surpassingly calm. Yet he did not seem foolish; there was the look of much care about him, but there was also a cool acceptance of the care. I had never seen a likeness of him save for some barbarous woodcuts in local gazettes, yet I knew on the instant who he was. There could only have been one such man in any army. Struck as I was by the strong repose of his face, I could not take my eyes off his hands, which were huge. I have been told that he could crack a walnut between his thumb and forefinger, and I readily believe it, for his hands were big even on his big frame. We had a stoneware maker in our company, Edward Kippen, whose great broad hands were the object of much comment and derision, and yet the man before me could have engulfed and hidden both Kippen's hands in one of his.

I jumped aside and raised my hand in a silly approximation of one of Captain Totten's dazzling salutes, and, scarcely glancing my way, the tall man touched his hat.

He rode past, and I went to find Jib and tell him of having seen the General. Jib was on his feet, the ague having passed for the while. He had managed to find another musket, a brother to mine and a sorry replacement for the beauty he had lost. I derived some petty amusement from this: "Why, you should have sent requesting your father to send you the handsome firelock that you offered me the morning after we signed up."

He shook his head and gave a dim smile, looking over his new weapon. "Perhaps I will have better luck with this one."

I told him that I had seen our commander in chief

and that he looked like a man who could win battles. Aaron Thane, overhearing me, growled some obvious observations about the deceit often inherent in appearances. "And besides," he said, "he's as rich as the king of England himself. I have no use for these rich Virginians. Treat you as though you should clean their boots with your tongue."

Jib suggested that Thane had never seen a rich Virginian. "Oh, I guess I know what they're like," said Thane. "And I saw Washington, didn't I, right after the battle, and he didn't save my skin on that hill — I did."

October passed away, its final days brightened by conversations like this one. On the last day of the month the army removed itself to the heights of North Castle, swinging back like a door on the hinge of our left flank, which stayed where it was, near to the enemy. We walked to our new positions through the lowering afternoon of Allhallows Eve. A mottled, fish-belly sky robbed the fallen leaves we trod of their luster. When we were settled in an unconvincing line, Captain Totten read us a general order issued by Washington which censured in the strongest terms the actions of certain officers who had used the confusion following the battle as an excuse to steal horses from nearby farms. For our supper that night, Sergeant Kite supervised the cooking of what he claimed to be a great treat. A large amount of weevily flour was cooked in a larger amount of fat until it congealed into a single cake, which was divided among us. I did not much care for it, but I nonetheless fared better than Sergeant Clew, who became even grayer and more somber than usual and eventually vomited up his meal. Evening came on with a high wind which drove cloud armadas fast across the close sky. Then the sky opened and rain poured down upon us all night long.

The next day Sergeant Kite set us about the task of building flimsy barricades. We rooted up cornstalks from the fields and piled them up with their dirt-clotted ends facing the enemy, in hopes of deceiving him into thinking that we had somehow built massive earthworks. It was light work, but disheartening; Sergeant Kite grumbled about "sham soldiers building sham fortifications."

This feeble bit of make-believe seemed to work, however. A couple of nights later we were awakened and called to our arms while a great stir went on in the enemy camp. We heard many commands and the noise of heavy wagons moving, and in the morning we saw that the British lines were empty. We indulged in some tentative self-congratulation and were read more general orders forbidding looting and the burning of dwelling places.

Nevertheless, that night we saw dwellings burning in White Plains village, and the next day we heard that a Massachusetts officer had set fire to the home of a helpless old woman and ordered her effects transported to his tent. When Ensign Bryce heard of this, he spoke to Lieutenant Godkin with uncharacteristic heat: "Now, that's a fine thing, a novel way to show our countrymen how we strive to secure their liberties." Lieutenant

Godkin concurred, calling it a "rascally" deed. This complaint was overheard by Sergeant Kite, who, with considerable forbearance, was teaching a few of us how to roll cartridges more expeditiously. "Oh, it's grand to be back in the army," he said. "Regular soldiers you are after all, pillaging with the best of 'em." I protested that we had one no pillaging, and Kite replied that that was because we had not been soldiers as long as the brave boys from Massachusetts.

More idle days passed, in which we were free to pursue the lusty pleasures of a soldier's life by wandering through the gaunt and gutted Tory village of White Plains. One of our company, Malachai Code, displayed a certain genius in being able to find a whore in the ruins of the village, whose favors he extracted for a few firecakes. My bowels were still affrighted, and the thought of a whore interested me not at all.

I did, however, feel considerable envy when I spied a gaggle of barefoot Massachusetts militia heading homeward. Their term of enlistment had expired, and happier men you never saw. They were all bones and grime, with the remnants of their clothing draped over their shoulders rather than fastened in any conventional way. Many had great sores on their faces, and all were emaciated, yet they passed by singing and skylarking. "Hello, you boys!" they called out to us where we sat watching them. "Keep the war hot for us, and we'll be back directly we've gotten fat and had babies and made our fortunes. Good-bye, and we'll see you in hell before we see you again in this army." One of them threw a fistful of cartridges our way, and another, evidently taking pity on us, tossed us a bottle of spirits. Of course, it turned out to be empty.

The jubilant little parade had just passed out of sight when Captain Totten approached us. "Here's great news, men," he called. He seemed so pleased that we all leapt up and clustered about him. There was not a man of us but hoped that some sort of peace had been effected or that, though an inconceivable miscalculation, our terms had also expired. But no. "I have just received word that at last we will be rejoining the 3rd Pennsylvania." We groaned, but Captain Totten talked on obliviously. "General Washington is soon to move back toward Manhattan, for there is a good chance that General Howe may lay siege to Fort Washington. It is a fine fort, utterly impregnable, I'm told, and the 3rd will be among those honored to defend it. We were taken unprepared the other day, but that will not happen twice." As usual, Lieutenant Godkin followed up Totten's announcement with some patriotic claptrap.

Pleased as Captain Totten may have been with our imminent absorption into the 3rd, the prospect held no joy for me. The men of the 3rd were not old comrades, I had no friends in the battalion, and I was certainly not anxious to rush into a siege. My wishes were not considered, however, and soon we were on the march to Verplanck's Point on the Hudson. There we crossed to Stony Point — a much easier crossing than the one to which Mr. Potter had treated us. The army, small though it was, was split up: some men would remain at North Castle with Major General Charles Lee (whose capacities I had heard much lauded — he had been a

British officer before resigning his commission to join the American army), and some were to guard the Hudson with Major General Heath.

There were not more than two thousand of us, then, who followed General Washington down the Hudson toward the fort that bore his name. A steady wind blew the last leaves off the trees, but the sky remained a deep scrubbed blue, and as long as we were on the march, we did not feel the cold too much. Every now and again I would catch a glimpse of General Washington, always from afar. "There he is," Aaron Thane would say. "Look at that popinjay on his big fat horse." Once he appended to this, "We do his fighting and eat rubbish, while he is getting rich from our efforts," to which Bryce replied, "Calm yourself, Thane, and quit your cawing. He is serving without pay, and, besides, it is a fine amount of fighting you've done for him." Thereafter, Thane also called Ensign Bryce a popinjay, when Bryce was out of hearing. The word became stuck in Jib's mind, and for a day or two he called everyone a popinjay. The fever had burnt a good deal of flesh off him, and his eyes were enormous in his head.

One cold, blowy, mid-November evening Captain Totten told us that our travels were nearly at an end. "Tomorrow we will reach Fort Lee, which is across the river from Fort Washington, so at last we will be with the 3rd." But once again he was wrong, for our destinies and those of the 3rd Pennsylvania were not to be intertwined.

Shortly after daybreak, we heard the sound of artillery. It was muffled with the distance so that it seemed to register itself as pressure deep inside the mechanisms of the ear, but it was heavy and constant. It was coming from the direction of the river, and Captain Totten had us moving that way in no time at all. As it was, it took us upwards of an hour to get there, and, despite the cold day, we were sweating and gasping when we arrived. Once there, however, we were free to take our ease and witness at our leisure the destruction of the best part of our army.

We came out along the wooded riverbank a few hundred feet to the north of the earthworks of Fort Lee and beheld Fort Washington half a mile distant on a rocky promontory high above the sparkling Hudson. Nature seemed to glory in our debacles, for, as at the White Plains, she had provided a perfect day. There were a few happy little clouds lolling like sheep in the benign sky, and all the world was blue and windy. Out in the river a frigate, her rigging sharp as a diagram in the clear light, heeled gently at the discharge of her guns. I had never seen a man-of-war in action, and the sight so absorbed me that it must have been a minute or two before my eyes strayed to the object of the ship's attentions. The fort looked sturdy enough, with its redoubts and entrenchments, and if the frigate was doing it any damage, I could not see it. A flag floated jauntily over the fort, and half a mile or so upriver from it, guns at a small redoubt returned the ship's fire, also causing no evident distress. A couple of skiffs were crossing between Fort Lee and Fort Washington, and I was worried that we should be taken over to join the incipient fight. But the morning wore on, and we stayed where we were, our officers looking through their spyglasses and talking with great animation.

"God, how I wish I were there," exclaimed Lieutenant Godkin again and again. Ensign Bryce grinned at Thane, who was nuzzling a piece of salt meat, and said, "Your sentiments too, eh, Thane?" Thane shook his head, and Jib said, "I certainly prefer the spectator's role."

"It's a fine day for a fight," said Totten. "And look at those works. I'd sooner storm the gates of hell. The British will have a surprise today."

So far there was no sign of British troops, though heavy musketry from the far side of the fort suggested they were present. Toward noon Lieutenant Godkin said, "There come the damnable hirelings." We could see some movement over near the redoubt that was firing on the ship. Soon there was fire and a great deal of smoke. At length the enemy broke off the attack, and we cheered.

"That must be the 3rd," called Totten.

A little while later someone spotted some officers, General Washington among them, returning across the Hudson to Fort Lee. "Getting out in the nick of time, most likely," said Thane, peering at the distant boat. But we were in high spirits and certain of the outcome. There was another attack on the redoubt, which again defended itself with spirit. Sergeant Kite, chuckling, reminded us that, had we not been "so full of piss and wind" on Chatterton's Hill, we could have acquitted ourselves as well as the men at the redoubt.

Then, sometime in midafternoon, the scene altered drastically. Tiny figures began to run for the protection of the fort from outlying entrenchments, and the British infantry appeared. There was another attempt on the obstinate redoubt, which held for a few minutes more. Then the attackers overran the position, and soon the fort was ringed by the enemy. After a while the gunfire ceased and the smoke began to dissipate.

"Oh, God damn it," said Captain Totten in a cool, minor tone. "Oh, God damn it to hell." For the flag had disappeared from its staff, and Fort Washington was in the hands of the enemy.

"How I wish I had been there," said Lieutenant Godkin.

"Oh, don't be such a silly ass!" shouted Sergeant Kite, and walked away from the surprised lieutenant.

A bulky officer rode by us quickly, his face contorted with what I took to be rage, but what I later ascertained was grief, for the man was Major General Nathanael Greene, whose earnest pleadings had convinced General Washington that the fort could be held.

Sergeant Kite turned on us and began chastising us as though we had surrendered the fort. "There's no damned reason for it. Rabbits could have held that position. Well, there's an end to this army and this war, for there were thousands of men in that fort, and cannon and all, and now they are gone forever." He pointed out across the river. "Those were trained men, regulars, and that's the best they could do; hold an unassailable position for three hours. And what do we

117

have left? You, and the likes of you. Over there we had nothing, and now we're left with less than nothing."

"That's enough of that, Sergeant," said Captain Totten. Sergeant Kite quieted himself and sat down on the ground, but even Captain Totten did not attempt to offer us any encouragement.

As the bitter afternoon waned, we saw the prisoners, hundreds of them, being marched out of the fort. After they were gone, an unexpected explosion nearby made me nearly jump out of my skin. It was one of the big thirty-two-pounders in Fort Lee. In futile rage, the gunners had loaded their pieces and were firing at the now hostile fort across the river.

"Much good that'll do 'em, poor bastards," I said.

"We are the poor bastards," said Jib.

8

Sergeant Clew

We camped that night in Fort Lee. All the next day and the day after, we heard and passed on gloomy rumors about the extent of the reverses. We were told that there had been some three thousand men in Fort Washington, and a multitude of fine cannon. We were told that General Washington had been seen weeping as the works were carried. We were told that several regiments were now considering going home, even though their enlistments were not up.

As for our company, now forever orphaned from the 3rd Pennsylvania, it kept to itself near Greene's men, and, God knows, nobody protested our presence, for thirty firelocks were thirty firelocks.

Sergeant Kite became so ill tempered that even the officers were shy of him. Captain Totten kept his own counsel, and Lieutenant Godkin was seen talking to himself. "That's one audience that will ever be pleased to hear what he has to say," said Thane. Jib succeeded in passing his fever along to four or five others, among them Corporal Curran, who roused himself from long periods of apathy to give vent to the most frightful obscenities.

The weather turned foul, with a cold gray sky constantly drooling down on us, so that we were always shivering and clammy. To add to the discomfort caused me by my unpredictable bowels, one of my shoes split open. It could still be used, but nothing can so provoke a feeling of total spiritual poverty as having a shoe open to the weather. As an old soldier of the great war for our independence, the only sure advice I can give any young man aspiring to a military career is: Keep your feet dry. I did have the grace not to complain about my leaking shoe, for most were worse off than I. Malachai Code had somehow contrived to lose a shoe at the White Plains and had whittled a ghastly-looking device out of wood to make up for the lack. This he tied to his foot with leather straps. He hobbled about on it and did not complain, so I saw that I could not very well fuss about my lot. And the worst of our company was in better shape than the best of the men around us, most at whom had been in the field since the spring. Many of them had no shoes at all, and a few times I spied one figure who was wholly naked save for the remnants of some flimsy linen drawers and a Hessian jacket that he had somehow acquired.

On the morning of our fourth day at Fort Lee we heard some smart musketry to the north, and the British were again upon us. I had been peering into the brackish depths of our kettle, trying to determine what was being cooked for breakfast, when the popping noise brought me up with a start. At the same instant, Major General Greene appeared on his horse, calling men to arms and out of the fort. I got barely a glimpse of him before Sergeant Kite was pushing me toward our stacked arms. "Here, here, grab your pieces! You know what to do — take your firelocks and run for your lives. Christ, how I love this new kind of warfare!" There was a great commotion of running, swearing men; Greene was going to try to hold no forts this day.

Captain Totten came among us, buckling on his sword and calling to Lieutenant Godkin to get us moving toward the Hackensack River. "British'll get there first," said Thane, but he was quick as the rest of us in leaving the fort. We ran by tents that were pouring forth men, who joined us in our flight. I passed a little group of wounded, who stretched out their arms piteously to their fleeing comrades, calling, "Don't leave us! Don't leave us behind!" But there was nothing for it, and we left them there. I made my way past strewn equipment and kettles still bubbling untended, and emerged from the fort.

The road that led toward Liberty Pole and thence to the river was hellish with jostling men. I saw Malachai Code fall down and, regaining his feet, tear off his clumsy wooden shoe and throw it aside. A moment

121

later he pulled off his good shoe and threw it away as well.

In a great press we made our way forward. Off to the right of us a frenzied gunner was beating two mules with a stick. The poor beasts strained at a brass six-pounder but could not budge it. Finally the gunner cut them loose and, abandoning the gun, led the animals onto the seething road. Along the way to Liberty Pole I saw at least a dozen cannon left behind for the British. We also passed by large herds of cows, which had been driven in from Maryland and Pennsylvania to feed us, and which would now feed our enemies.

We pushed on past the dismal and vacant village of Liberty Pole and came up against a crowd of men at New Bridge. Here I saw General Washington, who seemed more composed than I felt I should ever be again in my life. He exchanged a word or two with Major General Greene, who then galloped back the way we had come, presumably to gather up stragglers.

We crossed the bridge and, emerging on the other side of the Hackensack, felt for the moment the illusion of safety. After an hour or two of shuffling about, I heard a forlorn rattling. Drummers were tapping away, and we were formed into a column two abreast. At length we set out for Hackensack, where we arrived at dusk, with the rain coming down softly but steadily upon us. A few citizens peered disconsolately out at us from the comfort of their houses. My sprung shoe squeaked and squirted with every step I took. I had not had a bite to eat all day, but my bowels had worked nonetheless, with no way for me to control them and no time to stop to empty them. I was slick with mud from my eyes to my feet. For all my wetness, my throat was dry with the onset of fever.

Thus the army and I entered Hackensack. Had anyone told me that the army would still exist in a month's time, I would have laughed — or wept — in his face.

The next morning I found my fever had blossomed so that my bones ached and my teeth rattled. I lay awake with only my noisy jaws to keep me company, but not for long. Soon Sergeant Kite was kicking at my sleeping fellows and bawling at them to assemble. I got to my feet, and as soon as I did, I felt I was swaying like a tree in the storm, my head a bubble of bright gas prey to every shift of the winds. Kite got the whole company up while the rest of the army slept on. Having got us in line, Kite stood aside, and Lieutenant Godkin stepped out to have a word with us.

"Good morning, men," he said. "I know that it is no secret that I was once a schoolmaster. I found it a most worthy occupation and have no wish more ardent than to resume my duties. As a tutor, I have ever been open to the influences of great men, and so it is my privilege not to be wholly unacquainted with the works of Mr. Alexander Pope and Mr. John Milton."

"I'm glad I didn't sleep through this," muttered Aaron Thane.

I saw a tiny green spider picking its way up Lieutenant Godkin's boot, and giggled so loud and unexpectedly that I was not even sure I had made the

123

noise until Godkin turned toward me, pained. At this, I felt a surge of shivery pity for the man and resolved myself to be the most sober of the lot of us.

"I mention my acquaintance with these men," he went on, "because I have, from time to time and — though it ill befits me to say it — not wholly with approbation, also addressed myself to poetry. I have found solace in this quiet craft, and last night, perturbed by the events of the last few days, I again turned my hand to it. I was mildly pleased with the results, and it is my hope that you will be as well. I solicit your cordial attention."

He pulled from his pocket a piece of paper, unfolded it, and held it before him, peering at it with a cozy smile. Then he began to read from it in a big hollow voice while Sergeant Kite, with the bland face of the old soldier who has been an agent of even worse follies, passed among us, handing each a copy which Lieutenant Godkin must have written out the night before. I have long forgotten better verse, but I have that copy yet. It lasted out the war and the rest of my life; it is before me now, torn in the creases, with Lieutenant Godkin's irreproachable calligraphy faded to a warm faint brown:

> *O war, whose red and metal voice belies*
> *Constructive childhood's meek and docile cries,*
> *Stay thy intemp'rate hand and list this day*
> *To a* Lieutenant *who would have his say.*
>
> *I saw thy sanguine face at the White Plains,*
> *And in thy service scatter'd crimson stains*

That wash'd th' autumnal field a transient red
With liquor sapp'd from Britons *wrack'd and dead.*

I did not court this most odif'rous thing,
But came unwilling, spurr'd by a mock-king,
Who, waxing fat 'neath Empire's *gibbous moon,*
Vain sought to move my feet unto his tune.

I was no warrior, but a pedagogue,
Whose only task was to save from the bog
Of ignorance young men and guide them straight
To Learning's *far but opalescent gate.*

Then rose the tempest from the vasty North,
The brazen chariots of Mars *burst forth,*
And towns that once were sweet with blissful peace,
Were all affrighted, all without surcease.

A schoolbook soldier? Nay! I dropt my pen,
And walked the one road open to brave men,
With fens and thickets choking all its bends —
Yet I will sup on Vict'ry *ere it ends.*

He thrust his copy back into his pocket and grabbed hold of the handle of his sword, his face all in a courageous grimace. We stood before him in the dawn, sick and beaten and embarrassed. Then I fell down with my fever and woke to being kicked up again and marched to the Acquackanock Bridge, whose name I remember only because the fever made it rattle about in my head. We got there easily enough and crossed the Passaic River with no sign of the enemy. All the way, I trilled and babbled to myself, thinking that I had only to turn into this pasture or that road and I could pull open the door by its loose brass handle and be in the shop with my father and the watches. Then the steamy fantasy would dissolve and I would be walking a road with no available turnings, with Jib beside me. He was also mumbling to himself and, by the time my internal smoke cleared away late of a cloudy evening, he had composed an answer to Lieutenant Godkin's effusion.

He recited it around the fire that night to general plaudits, and never forgot it thereafter:

I am a soldier bold and true
In Washington's great army,
And though I've yet to win a fight,
This war does not alarm me.

I was not raised to shoot a piece,
But to be a ship chandler,
And if I chose to kiss a girl,
I fain knew how to handle her.

So bold in love, bold in the field,
I came into this service,
And if 'tis any cause at all,
It scarcely does deserve us.

My comrades brave and I with them
Ran fast before the Hessians,
And should bold Mars be on our side,
He'd best to make concessions.

We cannot fight, but we can run
From dawn until tomorrow,
And if our foes run half so fast,
They'll do it to their sorrow.

We'll run through swamps and over hills,
We'll leave 'em far behind us,
And if we ever turn to fight,
They'll be hard press'd to find us.

And if, bold Godkin, a real fight
Should ever come to pass, sir,
And if you want us in your line,
Why, stick it up your arse, sir.

We ended our march in the drab little community of Newark, passing around scraps of Jib's doggerel, carefully out of Godkin's hearing — this caution itself being an index of certain feelings we must have had for the man. The resourceful Malachai Code appeared with a loaf of sugar he had found in a store, still wrapped in its blue paper, which we shared. While we were sucking on the sugar, it began to rain — big spitty gobs at first, warmer than the air around us, and then colder and colder until we were all shivering. I forced myself to go to sleep with the heavy drops tapping like fingers on my cheeks.

It was still raining the next morning when Jib shook me awake with the news that Sergeant Clew was dead. I roused myself and went to where he lay wrapped in his blanket, staring up into the rain with waxy eyes. Ensign Bryce was poised above him. "Dead, by God," Bryce was saying as I approached. I made a good deal of noise coming over, so that Bryce turned his narrow face up to me. "Do you like that?" he demanded with foolish belligerence, and I replied foolishly, "Not very much."

127

I stared at Clew's face. He looked much as he had in life; that is to say, dead. "He died during the night," Jib said judiciously. We were all shocked by this ghastly kind of surreptitious death.

Sergeant Kite allowed as how he'd seen it before. "Last war," he said, "men died sometimes, just like that. It wasn't the food, or we'd all be dead."

Paul Bowen said, "He coughed a lot and said that he was cold last night. It is a sad thing, but he must have been sick."

"You damned fool," said Aaron Thane, "we're all sick. What's to keep the rest of us from dying in our sleep?"

"It happens sometimes," Kite said. "It's good luck for the rest of you; you'll be saved for the hangman."

By this time Lieutenant Godkin had appeared, full of plans for a burial, during which he orated at some length about how Clew had died "a sacrifice on Liberty's altar." When Godkin was through speaking, Thane said, "Now there's nobody left thinks Corporal Francis Curran is funny."

"I do, you whining bastard!" shouted Curran, disrupting what small effect Godkin's rhetoric had established. For once I might have laughed at one of Curran's remarks, but I saw the man was weeping. Jib said to me, "There is not a single aspect of this war that does not distress and frighten me." Captain Totten, his fine uniform black with the damp, spoke: "My boys, you have done well, and now we will devote the rest of this day to the solemn consideration of friends gone." And damned little else was there for us to do. We

128

walked the streets — or, more properly, street — of Newark, and watched the rest of the army come in. The men were in appalling condition, nothing but dirt and eyes. The one bit of incongruous splendor was to be found in the cannon, which, mired up to their hubs as they were, had nonetheless been washed slick by the rain and gleamed in the dull light.

The roads were a foul paste, the camp reeked, and we stayed in stinking Newark for the better part of a week. All that time the rain pissed down upon us, and hope corroded. Men deserted by whole companies. I was awake early the day after Sergeant Clew's funeral, as my head had rested in a little hollow in the ground while I slept, and the hollow had filled up with water. The first thing I saw was a large number of Connecticut men, their equipment on their backs, straggling out of the town chatting together, as though they were drifting away from a cockfight. Two or three officers struck poses and reminded the troops of their duty in thin voices, but the men flowed past them, laughing and chaffing.

Half an hour later an even larger group of Massachusetts boys walked off in perfect order, silent and determined. Their officers marched with them. A little later we saw yet more soldiers marching away. These, it turned out, were not deserting but had been ordered over to Monmouth County to suppress a Tory uprising there.

How I loathe the Jerseys! Even today I do my best to avoid a journey there, for the state of New Jersey is not only hideous of aspect but contains dire memories for me. Here we were to have our ranks fleshed out by a vast rally of Jersey militia, but scarcely a man showed up. On the other hand, when our enemies issued a general pardon to those who would sign an oath of allegiance, Jerseymen turned out by the thousands. All around us was flat, bleak, boggy country that fairly begged the rain to fall and make it yet more desolate. Every local with whom I had contact was wily and contemptuously fawning.

Nothing very good happened in Newark. By day I ate what cold and greasy provender I could scare up, and by night I was haunted by dire dreams in which things rose from the Jersey bogs to grab for me with hands and my mother came all moldy from the grave to peer at me with empty eyesockets. I was shaken awake from one of these dreams, early of a drizzly morning, by a man who seemed something of an apparition himself. He was slightly below middle height, with a great red droopy nose and startling eyes blue as the tropic seas. Cold and more weary than when I had gone to sleep, I demanded to know his business.

"Here, here," he said, "no call to be so surly. I was passing by and heard you cry out in your sleep and, from the expression on your face, judged the world you were in to be less pleasant than the one I roused you into. If I was mistaken, you may return to it."

I squinted up at the rain. "Faint chance of that, neighbor."

He produced some snuff and offered me a pinch. I shook my head, and he helped himself to it with enormous relish, smiling and making wet noises. "Ha, there, good. Oh dear, the snuff is a vice, to be sure, but at least a solitary vice." Corporal Curran, crouched nearby mending his jacket with what looked to be a handful of weeds, was quick to point out, loudly and with a vivid gesture of his hand, his idea of a solitary vice. The stranger turned his bright blue gaze on Curran. "The fleshly vices, sir, I am more comfortable practicing than discussing. But all such vices can undo but one or, at the most, two people. My partiality for snuff may give me catarrh, and a man and a woman may come to grief through license. But a nation will not suffer from catarrh through my individual fondness, nor through obscure couplings." He had given his unwelcome attentions back over to me. "A debauched ruler holding sway over a country gone hollow with rot can despoil a populace at his whim. We are all fortunate fellows, we soldiers who have yet the strength of purpose to smite such a ruler. Back to sleep then, friend, and do not dream of a despoiled past, but of a glorious time ahead, when, having passed through the bitter waters, we may drink of the sweet." With that, the optimist bounced to his feet and walked briskly off, pausing to have a word with Lieutenant Godkin, who greeted him as an old friend.

"Who was that cheery madman?" I asked Jib, who had come over during the fellow's discourse.

"Don't you know? Why, that man deserves our gratitude for helping to bring us to this place. I might have gone to my grave without once having viewed the splendors of Newark were it not for him and his book. That was Thomas Paine. He has been prowling around the camp telling us how lucky we are."

I thought of the winter before, when my father had brought home the copy of *Common Sense*, the ink still sticky on its pages. That very night I had taken a short walk to Polly's home, cursing the cold of a winter not half so severe as the one I was now weathering. Mr. Lycott had dismissed Paine with a dour grunt or two. And now, a year later, crouching in rags in Newark, I had talked with the fellow. I was bleakly amused to imagine Mr. Lycott's reaction to my keeping such bad company and rather pleasantly surprised to find that Paine himself was actually sticking by the men who represented the last twitch of the rebellion he had sought to bring about. I said as much to Jib, who dismissed my observation, saying that the man must be mad as a shot goose.

From time to time General Washington would ride through the camp, big and quiet upon a leopard-skin saddle blanket whose furry brilliance compromised his dignity in a pleasant way. Occasionally he was accompanied by an animated and enormously fat young officer. This was Henry Knox, his chief artillerist, whose bulk did not reassure Aaron Thane. "That lard-arsed young popinjay is ten years my junior," he thrice confided to me, "and where did he learn the art of gunnery? In his Boston bookshop, that's where. Perhaps in his reading he also came across the story of Icarus and can further help us by fashioning us wings, so we can fly away to safety."

132

Always the rain came down, so that one morning, when it ceased, I awoke with a start. It was very clear and still, with half of a wet sun showing over the horizon and the whole sky pink from its light. All around me men lay sleeping, save for a few distant souls squatting about a fire. The ground steamed, so that the sleeping men looked to be cooking in some infernal place. I got to my feet, a little awed by the lack of the champing, complaining, shuffling noise of the army. Curran lay curled up like a baby, his hands bent into weak fists, dreaming, no doubt, of jeweled Persian women who anointed him with oils and yearned for his crooked gaze. Beside him, Jay lay square on his back with his mouth hooked wide open. One last fly, which had survived the ravages of autumn, moved weakly up his chin. I brushed it off and, taking my firelock, walked toward the gummy road that led away from the camp. There should have been sentries posted on the road, but no one hailed me as I passed the last of the sleeping men and ventured beyond the familiar stench of the American army quartered at Newark.

The sun rose up with its illusory November warmth and, flashing in a thousand fens, transformed the disgusting countryside for a little while. I walked along, humming and muttering to myself, quite at peace, until I came to some outbuildings and then a neat house, some fifty yards back from the road. Beyond were the charred remains of a barn. The house was inhabited, for there was smoke coming from the chimney and a little white thing tumbling about near the door.

I was not in friendly country, but the stillness of the morning, my firelock, and the vestiges of my fever gave me courage, so I started toward the house. I was half-way there when the white thing began to emit a frightful keening noise and the door was snatched open. A woman ran out and picked up the white thing, which, aloft, turned out to be a child. I dropped my piece and carried it along by the muzzle, so that the stock trailed along the wet grass in what I hoped to be a harmless manner. The woman, holding the child, which had lapsed silent, stood watching my approach.

"Good morning!" I called. "And have you any bread for sale?"

"Not for sale," she said, "but you are welcome to it if you keep out of my house."

"It is a fine-looking house," I replied ponderously, "and I certainly would be distressed to take my dirty self inside it."

She gave me a smile with half her face, the other half and her eyes remaining grave. She was a tall woman with neatly kept hair, and she held herself stiffly, so that at first I thought her a good many years my senior. Then, gathering my mind for some pleasantry, I saw that she had a young face — no older, perhaps, than Polly's.

"Good morning," I said again. "I am Freelon Starbird, of Captain Totten's company of the Pennsylvania Militia, which is at Newark."

"Then I have much to thank you for," she said, "for your comrades burned my barn and took off a weak old cow that couldn't have survived the trip to Newark."

134

"Not my comrades," I said, "for I would call no man a comrade who would so disrupt the peaceful — "

She interrupted my graceful phrasing. "You're a pompous one. How old are you? Eighteen?"

"Older, thank you."

"I am Mrs. Collins. Here, look after Peter, and I will get you some bread, if you don't set my house afire while I'm about it."

She set the child down at my feet and went into the house. Peter Collins, a broad-faced little boy, seemed perfectly content to share the yard with me once his mother and I had exchanged words. He regarded me with solemn caution, and, this infant scrutiny making me uncomfortable, I sought to divert him by bending the small finger of my left hand to an extreme angle, an art I perfected when very young. When this failed to engage his interest, I augmented the feat by making a squeaking noise and contorting my face. Peter Collins remained unmoved by these wonders, so I crouched down to afford him a better view of them and, while so engaged, was interrupted by his mother's reappearance. Abashed at being caught in so undignified a position, I tried to leap upright and fell over on my back. Corporal Curran's sleeping mind may have been abroad, for I gave vent to a terrible obscenity, but Mrs. Collins seemed not a bit arrested by it. "Do not distress yourself, Mr. Starborn. Here is your bread."

"Starbird," I said. "And thank you."

Peter, at last pleased by some working of his childhood surroundings, stuck out his fat arms and shrieked with glee.

"That's a fine little fellow," I said, regaining a foot-hold in the world of men. I took the bread Mrs. Collins offered and bit into it. Although it was a day old, it was as sweet and soft a morsel as ever I had sampled.

"Thank you, and thank you, for I have these three months past been eating meat that would have served as bookbinding."

She laughed and crossed her arms over her bosom. "Sit down and finish it, then." So I sat down on a stone step and chewed away while Peter smiled and pointed at me. I was finished soon enough and made to pick up the child, but he quickly regained his initial suspicion and fled out of reach.

"Well, Peter is scared of soldiers," she said, "as well might he be."

"I am sorry for the barn, but I have learned the upsets of war for myself. I should at this very moment be fixing a watch, for that is my calling, and not approaching strangers in New Jersey, begging for food."

"You are not from New Jersey?"

"Pennsylvania, where my father is a most respected watchmaker."

"That sounds like a warm and quiet trade. What has brought you to my door clothed in mud?"

I garbled something about "the workings of Providence." She laughed at me and squeezed up her eyes in a nice way, and I saw that one of them was blue, and one brown.

"It must have been a very certain thing that took you from your last, or whatever it is that watchmakers make

136

watches upon. You must be very sure that you will win."

She spoke gently and mockingly, as most girls do at first, and I annoyed myself by apologizing for my presence and for my appearance. "Oh, no, I do not think we'll win. But I am happy to serve, secure in the knowledge . . ." — I carried on with some of the philosophy of my new friend Thomas Paine, which she attended with skeptical interest.

"Well, it seems most extraordinary," she said when I was through, "for Mr. Collins thinks that his cause will prevail, and never was there a more steadfast servant of the good King George. My husband went off to war on his horse in a lovely green uniform, and he would cut off your head given the chance. You'll hang, you poor scarecrow, when Mr. Collins and his friends see what you have done to his barn."

"His barn, but not his wife," I replied with some heat though not wholly annoyed, since she spoke of Mr. Collins' cause with the same irony she employed for mine, "since my fellows seem to have left you undisturbed in your person, while your husband's Hessian friends see fit to observe no such niceties." Then, since she still smirked, I threw in a barefaced lie: "My sister was raped and murdered by the Germans." I was immediately ashamed of myself for this stupid fiction, the more so when she regarded me with real compassion and began to talk of the horrors of war. This, however, led to a more general and pleasant discussion, which I pursued with enthusiasm until there was a stir on the

137

road and some swaybacked horses with shabby riders passed down it, followed by the vanguard of the army.

By this time black clouds had churned into the sky from the east, and rain was imminent again, the stillness of the clear dawn replaced by fluky winds. My companion and I watched the soldiers pass by, bare-shanked and stumbling, while the rain came on.

"I see," said Mrs. Collins, "that God does not temper his winds to these shorn lambs."

"They're leaving Newark."

"So there is some wisdom in your cause," she said, smiling at me. Peter had bumbled into the house, and his mother and I stood in the lee of it and looked at the Army of Independence passing by before us. First there came a few men who walked like soldiers, though they had no uniforms. With them went the music of "Yankee Doodle," and they marched straight to the foolish air. They were followed by a rabble, many among it without any visible weapons. I did not see General Washington, but I did see fat Knox, followed by four or five cannon, and then more rabble and, incredibly, a few women, ostensibly employed to do the washing, still tagging doggedly along after men who must have been paying for their services with corncobs and lies. After that there was nothing but the rain, and then a peddler with his cart, and then more soldiers walking like soldiers, with their firelocks on their shoulders.

Then our company came into view and I heard Jib

calling, "Look, lads, there's Freelon, all settled down and farming in New Jersey. He'd be better off dead!"

"Fall in, Starbird!" yelled Sergeant Kite in a clear, jolly voice. "We've just won a great victory and you'll miss out on the plunder."

A man I'd never seen before, in bright red-and-white-striped pants, waved his hat exultantly. Thane, walking behind him, shouted, "Come along! We're off to the Delaware. There's ten American sail of the line waiting for us there, just up from the Carolina coast."

"That's right!" called someone else. "And Marlborough's come back from the dead to lead the army of Virginia up to us, and there'll be a big victory."

"Ho, Freelon!" — Jib again — "You'll want to share in the spoils if you hope to spend your age on a Jersey dungheap with your lass and glass."

I saw Captain Totten and Lieutenant Godkin walking backward, trying to keep the company quiet, and of a sudden I felt a deep regard for all of those dingy people out on the road.

"It's a wonderful sight, Mr. Starbird, an army with banners," said Mrs. Collins. "And I suppose you had best join them."

"I suppose I had, and I thank you again for your bread and your courtesy."

I started toward the road while she waved and, smiling, said, "Scant courtesy. But I suppose it is enough so that my husband's friends will burn my house for it. Good fortune to you, Starpen."

I made for the road and fell in with the company.

Corporal Curran, of course, was full of speculation as to how I had spent the morning.

Jib informed me that the army had fled Newark with the British fast approaching. The weather grew worse, and clouds of fog breathed across our column, so that it seemed as if the sopping sky had come right down to rest on our shoulders.

At Brunswick we once again had cannonballs about our ears as we filed out of one end of the town while the British entered the other. They would have snuffed us out then and there, had not some provident soldiers damaged the bridge across the Raritan. As it was, the British unlimbered their guns and commenced a smart cannonade, which was answered by a couple of our cannon commanded by a frail, girlish-looking officer who seemed to know what he was about. There had been some talk about our making a stand along the Raritan, but the advent of the enemy blew such fancies clear away.

"Keep moving, keep moving," said Sergeant Kite. "This army is like the French navy — it is too precious to be put in the way of getting hurt." The balls fell about us, throwing up sudden explosions of mud as they skipped along the ground, but executing no damage that I could see.

We made our way before the enemy as fast as we could, for by this time the British and Germans had grown in our regard until they were invincible, as little prey to human frailties as the weapons they carried. Always they were just a few hours behind us, tall and clean and happy in their bright uniforms, covering the distance between us in huge strides, their bayonets glittering like Greenland spar. So we fled, in our squalid little regiments, from those hardy, well-fed men whose only job was to kill us.

Our numbers dwindled daily. Sentries were posted on the roads about our camp to check deserters, but there was precious little a sentry could do when a whole regiment came his way. At the end of November the Maryland militia went home, along with scores of New Jersey soldiers. And of course there was always a steady trickle of men leaving by twos and threes.

On the other hand, there were some hopeful rumors about General Charles Lee's troops, which we had left after the White Plains. With the catalogue of defeats behind us, his balance had risen while General Washington's had sunk. Aaron Thane was not alone when he loudly spoke the virtues of Lee and the folly of Washington. "A true British general come to our cause fresh from triumphs in Europe, and who do we have commanding us? A popinjay Virginian who fought one battle before this war and lost it. Where is the reason in that?"

"Well, what's an Englishman doing in our army in the first place?" Jib asked Thane after one such declamation.

The query annoyed Sergeant Kite. "We were all Englishmen up until last summer, Grasshorn," he snapped.

"Anyway," said Thane, "do you know what I think?"

"God, yes!" said Jib. "We all know what you think."

"I think," Thane persisted, "that our fine general is keeping Lee and his men away because he's jealous of him. He knows that Lee can do a better job. That's what I think."

"And a damned stupid thought it is," said Kite. "General Washington is not fool enough to kiss away thousands of men for a matter of pride."

"We'll see if it's nonsense," cried Thane, "when we're all dead and in the ground from George Washington's bumbling."

"At that time," said Bryce mildly, "I expect that we shall see that everything is nonsense."

Whatever the reason, the days went by with no sign of Charles Lee and his legions.

The last of the tents had been burned and abandoned when the army left Brunswick, which gave Thane some pleasure, since we had never benefited from them. Mostly we slept on the ground, but one night we put up in the dank comfort of Nassau Hall in the College of New Jersey at Princeton. This amused Ensign Bryce, for only the year before, he had been a scholar there. "When I think on it," he said, "I'm not sure that I don't prefer running for my life to the study of oratory."

The town of Princeton, like all the other towns we passed through, was haggard and deserted, the scholars gone and many of the inhabitants vanished as well.

Shortly after we left Princeton, leaving a few pioneers behind to fell trees in hopes of impeding the progress of our pursuers, a man up ahead of our company found a large pumpkin, which he held aloft impaled on the muzzle of his musket. It bobbed along ahead of us in the half-light of the storm, and we followed the foolish vegetable, a rout of specters driven south by west across the Jerseys.

9

Lieut. Godkin

We came at last to the banks of the Delaware, where there was great bustle and confusion, for of course the British were expected momentarily. It was frighteningly cold along the river; a wind heavy with moisture blew steadily, forming strange, brief sculptings on the gray water. For once our leaders appeared to have prepared for a contingency, and the river was crowded with boats of every description. Someone had taken care to see that the craft were waiting upon our arrival, although God knows that it did not require enormous military wisdom to foresee that we were to be chased out of the Jerseys. Down at the landing everyone was screaming and jostling. An officer, knee-deep in the water, was supervising the loading of a six-pounder upon a raft not much larger than the gun itself.

"Get in the water, you babies!" he shouted to three or four men who were leaning gingerly out, trying to lash down the piece without getting wet. As the men reluctantly complied, one of them stumbled against the raft, thereby tilting it enough so that the cannon, after a couple of indecisive lurches, rolled majestically into the river. "Oh, sweet Jesus! Oh, you clumsy bastards!" the officer yelled, dancing a jig in his rage.

"There now," called one of the men impudently. "Don't worry yourself, sir, for I am not hurt."

"You will be, if that piece isn't up on the bank at once. Here, take up that line . . ."

Near the frantic officer, an unusual boat was putting out for the opposite shore with a load of soldiers, and another like it was edging in to take aboard some horses. They were galleys, perhaps fifty feet long, with double banks of oars and large cannon mounted in their bows. Both were painted a jaunty combination of black and yellow. I wondered for a moment at their purpose and then realized that we had a navy on the Delaware. "Look, Thane," I called, remembering the enticement he had voiced to part me from Mrs. Collins, "there are your ten ships of the line."

"Indeed," said Thane, studying the beamy vessels. "If only they could coax Black Dick Howe's ships into action, we'd soon be finished with this struggle."

Our company did not cross with the navy, but in a number of small skiffs. As we were being rowed across, Jib and I stared at the Jersey shore, now nearly empty of men and equipment. A final gun was being trundled aboard a galley, and less than a hundred men waited to follow us. "It looks," said Jib, "as though we're going to be chased right back home. We're not far from Philadelphia now."

"Captain Totten tells me that we have secured all the boats there are on the river, so that they'll not be able to cross it."

The man who was rowing, a battered fellow with white hair, looked up at this. "That's right," he said, "and so they won't — until the river freezes over."

The shore we were approaching was thick with bare trees and scrubby winter bushes. "It looks as dreary as the Jerseys."

"It couldn't be," said Jib.

We disembarked and looked back across the river to where the British were making their punctual appearance. The last of the boats had gotten off, so the army was, for the moment, out of harm's way. The redcoats came down to the landing, and one of their officers gave us a disdainful wave of his hat.

Jib stood next to me, leaning on his musket, and I wondered at the changes that had been wrought in him since we had last stood together on Pennsylvania soil. His fever had burned all the surplus meat off him, and his bluster was, if not vanished, much diminished. So with the rest of the company. Malachai Code's feet, naked now despite attempts he had made during our long retreat to fashion some sort of protection for them, were swollen and blue, and scarred with ugly purple cuts. Corporal Curran, too, was worn to the blade. Paul Bowen looked to be full of health — some men seem to have impregnable constitutions, which adversity serves only to hone — but his jacket was gone, and he was wrapped in his blanket. Captain Totten still carried himself with an air, although his uniform was a parody of its former splendor, with all the pretty gold fixings gone from it. Lieutenant Godkin, burning with the fervor of our cause, yet appeared physically unable to support it much longer. Aaron Thane, roasting a bit of meat on his ramrod, moved with the chary motions of exhaustion, too weary, it seemed, even to complain. All of us were of a profound pallor under streaks of old grime, and all of us had colds or worse. We expended most of our breath in coughing and spitting.

Of course, the rest of the army, with months more in the field behind it, was in far worse condition.

"We look pretty shabby," I said to Jib.

"Yes, and much good have the exertions that brought us to this state done us."

We all settled down for the night, lying close together with our feet toward the fire. The British had begun to toss cannonballs at us from across the river, but we were too done in to pay them much heed.

Whatever momentum had enabled us to totter across the Jerseys was dispelled by our arrival into temporary safety. Perversely, our spirits guttered all the more as we crouched in the bushes on the banks of the Delaware. We were dreadfully uncomfortable and irascible.

Our second day there, Malachai Code attempted to teach us an obscure game of chance that, he claimed, had a wonderful potential to speed the leaden hours on their way. It involved an arrangement of sticks and had a name like "Guano." In any event, we never did quite master it, but it was a wellspring of ill feelings. We did not have any money with which to gamble, but rather matched possessions. Corporal Curran, at one point, put up a dog-eared pamphlet containing amatory verse and illuminated with woodcuts showing glum people performing the act of love, against a single glove that Jib had found somewhere. Jib did not much want the pamphlet, nor Curran the glove, but there was a fearful row over the outcome of the contest. Curran accused Jib of cheating. "How could I," demanded Jib, "when I do not apprehend the point of this wretched game? You are merely courting trouble, and you are a foul monkey of an Irish pimp."

"I would charge you dear for that, but I would not suffer myself to be touched by your fungulous hands." This was in reference to a strange, oozy malady that Jib had somehow contracted on the backs of his hands. "Look at those hands and be warned, boys: Never tamper with your mothers."

"You called your mother a whore when you were in your fever," said Jib, "but I thought it an Irish custom and not remarkable. But perhaps your mother was indeed remarkable, since other Irish women I've seen had not the wit for the calling . . ."

Curran leapt upon Jib, scattering the elements of Code's game, and the two thrashed about in an awkward fight while the rest of us witnessed this diversion with delight. Soon Lieutenant Godkin came over, demanding to know what the scuffling was about. Jib and Corporal Curran disengaged themselves and regarded each other sulkily while Lieutenant Godkin, gesturing toward the river, said: "There is your enemy, and it is he whom you should fight, not each other."

"Well, Lieutenant," said Thane, "had you kept your peace, we would at last have witnessed an American victory."

Before long it began to snow, and we moved upriver a bit to a place no more satisfactory than the one we had quit. The snow came down upon us for a day and a night, and then we had a fair day when it all began to melt. Lieutenant Godkin set us to building shelters, but, though we sorely needed them, there was a lethargy upon us and little was done. I made myself a shallow ditch, with a couple of fenceposts laid down in front of it to draw the teeth of the wind.

It became brutally cold, colder than any weather I could recall. The melting snow froze, and the ground beneath it froze. There was typhus in the camp, and men died and had to be left unburied on the iron ground. The wind burned my face and hands. It was exhausting, that cold, for my body was ever tensed against it as though I were laboring under a heavy burden. I ached and twitched, and my eyes ran and the tears froze on my face. Lying in my trough as I would have lain in my grave, I tried not to shiver, for, in shivering, I would let in the wind through a dozen rents in my clothing. At length I would be driven to quit my ditch and run toward the fire that we kept burning, so that I could warm first my front and then my back. Here I would scorch some food and eat it. We had more food than we had had during the retreat, for wagons were beginning to come out from Philadelphia with provisions. However, the dearth of clothing and blankets remained severe.

The change in my diet was enough to start my bowels griping anew, worse than before. Jib's fever had returned, and he lay by the fire, speaking only to beg that he not be taken to the hospital. In truth, the hospital was no place for a sick man. There the men lay side by side, mostly unattended, wanting medicines that had not been available since the sunny days on Long Island.

I was huddled by the fire one evening, watching the other fires that kept the army alive growing brighter as night came on, when Ensign Bryce approached accompanied by a stranger in a heavy coat. "This is Lieutenant Beard, of the Philadelphia Militia, who brings us the good news that reinforcements are arriving hourly from our city." But Lieutenant Beard, all swallowed up in his wonderful coat, did not have so happy a view of things.

"Oh, yes, reinforcements," he said. "But not many of them, and what good they'll be is beyond speculation. Not one in my lot has had any training, and damned little have I had."

"How did you leave things in Philadelphia?" I asked.

"I left with pleasure, for it is a city of the dead. The public presses are stopped, stores are abandoned, and gangs of cutthroats patrol the streets nightly. Everybody who could has fled to the country, and now that I see what we have guarding the approach to the city, I can scarcely blame them. It's wretched there; when I left, Congress was about to move to Baltimore . . ."

"The devil!" said Ensign Bryce. "Congress fleeing too?"

"Oh, yes, and it's a wonder they haven't left long before. Everybody gave up the city for lost when we got word of how things were in the Jerseys. A fine job you all did."

This startling burst of scorn from one who had done nothing whatever annoyed me and, I am sure, the rest of us. Yet we had been so chastened by the last couple of months that no one uttered a protest.

"So there you be," the obnoxious Beard went on. "We've got some cobblers and such out from the city with their firelocks, and not a soldier among 'em. Oh, and I understand you're to have your last days enlivened by the Philadelphia Light Horse, a bunch of foppish young macaronis who fancy playing at dragoons. They'll be around until they get cold, I suppose. Well, I'll be about my futile chores. Good evening to you."

He stalked off, leaving Ensign Bryce, shoulders peaked against the wind, peering after him. "Well, Thane," he said at length, "that man must be related to you. It grieves me that we did not enjoy his company while we were getting clear of the Jerseys."

Thane scowled and picked at a scab on his neck.

"If Philadelphia is lost," said Paul Bowen, "what will there be left worth defending?"

"Nothing," said Thane, "but our skins, which we ought to consider. We can all see the shape of things clear enough. I say it's time to follow the example of better soldiers than we'll ever be, and head for Philadelphia. I'd rather be there than here when the British

151

come. We have all had enough of this folly."

Lieutenant Godkin had risen to his feet during Thane's pragmatic musings. His large nose had been peeled of its skin by the wind, and it gleamed red in the firelight. "Thane," he said in a slow, conversational way, "you are no kind of a soldier and not much of a man, and I'd be no sorrier than the rest of us to see you back in Philadelphia. Nevertheless, if you take one step to implement your treason, I will kill you. I will kill you with my sword and be happy to do it. Every man in this command will stay until his term is up."

Thane muttered, "Go off and write a poem, you popinjay," very softly, and ceased his paltering. Jib was convulsed by a bout of coughing. When it had subsided, he lay on his side with ropes of phlegm hanging from his chin, staring at Lieutenant Godkin as though trying to decipher a message of great import hidden in the schoolteacher's face.

The next day, as cold as the one before, was interrupted in its course by devastating news. "Here it is," Sergeant Kite told us. "I've just got word that the precious General Lee has somehow contrived to get himself captured. That's right — captured. No, not fighting: he was mucking about in a tavern, miles away from his troops, and some British horse nipped up and grabbed him. It's a nice piece of soldiering, and one, Mr. Thane, of which your much despised General Washington has yet to be guilty. So God knows what is to happen now."

We knew, though, what was to happen. Many in our army were sick, and the army was the feeblest ghost of its old, none too effective self. Even those who were left would not be around for long, for the enlistments of virtually the whole army would expire with the old year. Our company's enlistments would not be up until the eighth of January, and during those few days, it seemed, we would be most of the Grand Army.

Perhaps George Washington's cripples would be destroyed by the British before the year was out, or perhaps they would be spared to walk away on the first of January — those who could walk. In either event, our remaining near the turbid Delaware was little more than a forlorn gesture. We knew this, yet there we stayed as the old, bad year of 1776 dwindled away in mortal days.

10

a Hessian

Happy Christmas, Freelon," said Jib to me on a cheerless morning. The sun was a white glow behind the eastern clouds, painful to look upon, but providing a dispirited light that cast no shadows and little warmth.

"It was happier a year ago." Then I had taken supper with my father and uncle and had consumed most of a fine pig, after which I went to visit Jib, whose father, with a huge amount of ceremony, had the audacity to pour us a thimbleful of wine. Afterward, full of some stronger spirits that Jib had smuggled into us, we had gone to call on the Lycotts, where the relatives quacked at us, and Polly was flushed with the heat emanating from the fire and the room full of people.

"Well, take heart from the fact that it is hardly likely to be worse next year."

"On your feet, my Christmas martyrs!" shouted Sergeant Kite, and the company formed two shaky lines. During the night the wind had shifted around, and now it boomed down on us from the north. About us the army was stirring, and other companies were falling into line.

"Orders," said Kite, and Captain Totten stepped forward.

"Men, I have just been speaking with Brigadier General Mercer, and I come with great news." Since our arrival at the Delaware, we had been camped near the men of Mercer's command, and I had often seen Mercer, a round-faced Scot, in conversation with Captain Totten. What great news Mercer might have for us was beyond my imagining, unless he had been able to secure us some clothing.

"We have long been chased and harried," Captain Totten continued, "but that is all done with now. Our turn has come around, and tonight we are going to strike the enemy."

Aaron Thane yelped like a dog, and Jib and I stared at each other. There had been rumors enough about some sort of action, but we had assumed that our operations would, of necessity, be confined to brief nighttime forays by small patrols.

"Not ten miles hence, at Trenton, are the very same Hessians who drove us from the hill at the White Plains. The Germans make a deal of Christmas, and they will swill their liquor tonight. At dawn they will be logy and stupid, and we will set the tune for them. We will cross the Delaware at dusk and march inland to Trenton with General Mercer's brigade. Every man will carry three days' cooked rations and forty rounds. This will be a glorious day for our cause."

We were dismissed to make our preparations. Thane had much to say about our coming adventure. Mocking Totten's voice, he squeaked, " 'A glorious day for our cause. . . . Great news.' Madness! We couldn't hold the Hessians for two minutes when we were strong and well and behind a wall and they were coming uphill at us — how are we going to get them out of a town? It was all we could do to get out of Trenton alive, and now we're going back to get our eyes shot out. Surprise them? The only surprise about this army is that there's any of it left. I knew this war would be the death of me. Madness! Vainglorious Washington knows he has us to play with for another week only, and so he wants to throw us away and have done with it. And we'll never get there in time anyway; look at that sky, it's going to storm for fair."

In this last he was indisputably correct, and in fact at dusk it began to snow, a hard powder that blew at us like sand. By this time we had been paraded down to the landing, called McKonkey's Ferry, along with Mercer's brigade, which was made up mostly of men from Massachusetts, Maryland, and Connecticut. There was such confusion at the landing, with units all mixed together and seething about, that I did not think we would ever be able to get across. And, when I got a good look at the river in the waning light, I was sure that we could not. The water was rushing by, bearing on its breast sheets of ice that ground together, making odd ceramic knocking noises at one moment and chittering, squeaking ones the next. Nevertheless, the passage was being attempted, for I saw boats out on the river heading for the far shore, which was already ghostly with the dusk. I recognized the vessels at once as Durham boats, for I had seen them often on the Delaware. They were about fifty feet long, and very wide and shallow, useful for bringing iron ore down from the Jerseys and, it now appeared, for carrying doomed armies to their destruction.

A New Englander near us who was also watching the boats turned to Aaron Thane. "Those big canoes there," he said, "are manned by Glover's men, and there's none better. Marblehead fishermen, Grand Banks boys; then the British said they couldn't fish any more so they took to killing British. Saved the army on Long Island, they did, and don't I remember it. We'd been knocked from pillar to post and were only waiting for somebody to come along and take our surrender, when a fog came down and they came in with their boats and whisked us over to New York. They're as comfortable on the water at night as a Frog dancing master at a cotillion . . ."

But the loquacious fellow had picked the wrong listener in frightened, angry Thane, who said abruptly: "I do not recall seeking your views on anything, you horse-faced buffoon."

The New Englander smiled at him for a moment and then spat squarely in his face. "There, neighbor; now

157

keep a civil tongue in your head or I'll stir your guts for you." Thane turned away, and the New Englander spoke to me. "He's scared, I suppose. Well, small wonder, for this is a scary business. I've been mostly scared, except when I was too sick to be, ever since I joined this army. But I've never been so scared as I am now; this is a mad business. Well, good luck, neighbor."

"Good luck," I said, and he left to climb into a boat with the rest of his company. I watched him take his place and noticed, as he climbed over the gunwale, that he had no shoes. When I glanced at the ground where he'd been standing, I saw that the trodden snow was pink with his blood. "Thank God for my shoes, holes and all," I said to Jib. "That poor fellow's feet are bleeding already, and he yet has ten miles to go."

Jib was shivering but had gotten the best of his fever. "Not a word out of him about it either. Well, it has been my experience that New Englanders are not quite human. It's rough country up there, and I suppose they eat gravel or something to stay alive. But," he went on, taking in the dim turmoil around us with a sweep of his arm, "this marvelous evening is well worth keeping alive for."

Our company was moved back a little from the river while a regiment of Virginians embarked. We waited near some artillery, and I noticed the girlish-looking officer who had covered our retreat from Brunswick with his guns. He appeared to be about twelve years old and was standing oblivious to the worsening storm, his hat pulled down over his pretty face. Every now and then he would pat one of his guns in an affectionate, familiar way, as if it were a favorite dog. Years later, when I heard more about him, I realized that this slender being was Alexander Hamilton.

Down at the landing, fat Henry Knox was bellowing instructions in the largest voice I have ever heard. If ever I have cause to enter into an argument with God, I would want such a voice to plead my part. Loud as they were, his words were perfectly distinct and laced throughout with a sort of glee, as though there was no better fun in the world than screaming in a snowstorm.

"Mercer! Mercer!" he was shouting. "Come along with your boys! You've got the next dance!" We shuffled down to a waiting boat. A rough-looking fellow in a round jacket with big leather buttons pulled me aboard. "Get in and get down, friend," he said, and reached for Corporal Curran, who stepped knee-deep in the icy water and came aboard swearing horribly. The boatman took a second to listen to him and nodded when Curran was done. "Not bad, not bad," he said, helping Jib aboard. Lieutenant Godkin climbed in, wearing a piece of paper folded up in his hat. I noticed that all the officers had, in fact, made use of this smart military effect to distinguish themselves from the rank and file in the darkness.

When we were all packed into the boat, Glover's men poled us away from the shore. At once the intensity of the wind doubled, and we were drenched with spray. The ice barked and scraped around us, and I watched it spinning past, each cake marked out by white froth. One particularly large cake drove in upon our bow and dealt the boat a terrible thump that swung it half around. We heeled over and shipped a mass of water that came in glossy and solid, and swashed over our feet. The cursing boatmen brought us back on an even keel again. At that moment the clouds parted and the moon shone down, throwing a luminous canopy over and about us. The gaunt light, flickering with the snow, illumined the whole breadth of the river, the men massed on both banks, a dozen boats motionless, black upon the black water. Then the clouds pressed in over the moon, the scene was obscured, and we were again in darkness, with the ice knocking against us and the boatmen grunting at their oars.

At last we felt a scraping on the bottom of the boat, and we were back again in New Jersey. As I made my way up the bank, I found that my clothing had frozen, so that it crackled as I walked.

A little way up from the landing Jib nudged me and I looked to see General Washington standing wrapped in his cloak, watching the desperate nocturnal traffic.

Some years ago I read a book by a hayseed parson named Weems, which purported to be a factual narrative of the life of George Washington. It is filled with old-maidish commentary and moral instruction, drawing on "examples" from Washington's life. One of these has him flopping down on his knees in the snow of Valley Forge and beseeching the Almighty to favor his noble cause. God only knows what harm this twaddle will do his memory when schoolboys gag over it, but I will tell you that the man I saw watching our disembarkation never spent much time on his knees.

Captain Totten called to us to salute Washington as we filed past. The tall man nodded and touched his hat. By now the snow had turned to sleet, which felt as though it were marking me with a thousand tiny cuts. I kept putting my fingers to my face to see if they would come away bloody, but they never did.

"Line up, line up!" called Sergeant Kite. "Lieutenant Godkin has something to read you."

"Good," said Jib. "I don't think I could carry this through were it not for a poem."

But Jib was mistaken. Lieutenant Godkin stepped forward holding a broadside and told us that Thomas Paine had produced a new tract, which he had been ordered to read to us.

" 'These are the times that try men's souls . . .' " he began, and I realized at once that I had overheard fragments of this oration being read aloud by the officers of other companies for the last two days. " 'The summer soldier and the sunshine patriot will, in this crisis, shrink from the service of his country; but he that stands it *now*, deserves the love and thanks of man and woman. Tyranny, like hell, is not easily conquered . . .' "

It was a wonderful harangue, and I can truly say that we, who above all others should have found little but irony in it, listened and were stirred.

" 'Heaven knows how to put a proper price upon its goods; and it would be strange indeed, if so celestial an article as *Freedom* should not be highly rated.' "

This was portentous stuff, well suited to Godkin's rich style, and while he read, we watched the boats

161

yielding up their shabby cargo. The path leading up from the landing was icy from the sleet now, and many slipped and fell, but they picked themselves up and kept going, some using their muskets for canes. A particularly naked boatload of men started up from the shore, one of them wearing only a hunting shirt, so that his thin legs shone naked as he passed by a small fire. I watched him struggling along while Godkin finished reading the broadside, and felt a wonder, not unmixed with pride, at being one of the inept men who were about to embark on this absurd project.

When Godkin put away the broadside, we did not cheer, but neither were any of us, even Thane, moved to mockery. The spirit of the oration ran through me for a moment like a swallow of brandy and dissipated itself just as quickly, leaving me feeling the more vulnerable to the weather. The wind rattled the branches of the trees around us; the sleet changed to rain and then back to snow, small flakes that fell hard enough to be audible, a sibilant, cautioning noise.

The crossing was unbearably slow. We were to have started for Trenton at midnight, but by the time the new day was two hours old, the artillery was still coming over. We were formed up in marching order, but no order to march was given. Thane complained a bit about our giving the enemy a fine surprise, wandering into their camp at midday when all were up and about, but he did not complain much, for it was too cold to waste any effort. I had become obsessed with keeping the snow off the back of my neck. It would build up on the collar of my jacket and melt against my neck, and when I shifted, icy water would spill down my spine. There seemed to be nothing I could do to stay this process, yet I never got used to it; every time I felt that chill splash of water, I'd jump and squeak.

Some boys in gallant red capes, whom I supposed to be members of the Philadelphia Light Horse, rode by us. Thane thought them popinjays. Then, at last, artillerymen in their black coats drove their guns past us toward the head of our waiting column. The cannon had torches fastened to their carriages, and these hissed and sparkled as they went past. Thus reminded of fire and warmth, I yearned for my shallow hole on the other side of the Delaware; my room and bed in Philadelphia were too remote and dear even to bear thinking on.

The column roused and shook itself, orders ran back, and Kite said, "Shoulder your firelocks. Pick 'em up, boys, and keep your ranks close. You don't want to be off after berries this night."

I took a step forward and nearly fell over, but after a while I fell into a sort of shambling rhythm. I could see the torches on the cannon, far ahead, lighting up the lower branches of the trees that lined our path. Once, after a long time, I nearly dozed but brought myself up sharply by shifting my grip on my firelock. The metal near the muzzle had become so cold that it burned the skin off my fingers. I sought to find the warm place where I had been holding it before, but could not, and thereafter the firelock seemed barbarously cold and heavy.

A minute or two after I fetched myself up against the freezing hot metal, Sergeant Kite, who had been floating back and forth through the company, appeared at my elbow and slapped me hard upon the back. "You're fine, aren't you, Starbird?"

"Yes. Why?" I asked.

"Oh, you made a big noise, but I can see you're fine." I thought that I had disengaged my fingers in silence, but all through the march I had been hearing whimpers and gaspings, loud and ingenuous, as if those who uttered them were crying out in their sleep. I supposed it was not remarkable that I should have been responsible for one such noise.

The only pleasant thing about pain is that, once endured, it cannot be recalled. I remember that I vomited up a thin fluid upon myself, but I cannot remember any of the accompanying sensations. Once Jib fell over, heavily and solidly, in midstride, and two of us had to lift him to his feet, and he remembered that not at all. I remember playing little games of counting my footsteps. I did not know that I was counting aloud until Curran told me to be quiet. Once I dropped my firelock; it made a loud noise on the icy road, and the man behind me fell over it. I retrieved it and helped him up, and he cursed me and I him for an hour. At the end of our cursing, I was talking about the differences between clock- and watchmaking, and he about a horse he had once owned. Nor do I remember which of my companions it was with whom I exchanged these ravings.

But for the most part we walked in silence, slipping frequently on the road, which was in spots smooth as glass. Once Washington rode down the column, calling out, "Press on! Press on, boys!"

At length we reached a dark hamlet, where we were called to a halt. "Eat now," said Kite. "We'll be moving on in a minute." There was some commotion behind us. "That will be Sullivan's men," Captain Totten explained. "They'll be marching along the river road; we're going inland. Hit the Germans from both sides, and there'll be nothing left of 'em. Greene's taking our corps."

"Greene," said Thane, doubtless thinking of Fort Washington, but too weary to make more of the matter.

When we were ordered to resume the march, it was discovered that Jib had fallen asleep sitting upright, with his rations clasped in his hands. We had some difficulty rousing him. I pursued my weary trudging and gradually was able to distinguish the figures limping along in front of me, and the snowy trees beside the path. So dawn was coming, and we were nowhere near Trenton. Again we halted briefly, and I saw General Washington approaching, grave and haggard. All down the column he spoke to the men, and as he passed by us, he said, "Men, stick by your officers. For God's sake, stick by your officers."

Now, too tired to go much farther or to care if I didn't, I resumed the march, and after another hour or so we reached Trenton.

By then the sleet was coming down again, mercifully at our backs. The column ahead began trotting, and Captain Totten ordered us to do so as well. "Oh,

God," moaned Jib, but he picked up his feet with the rest of us, and we all began loping; every footfall jarred my skull. Up ahead we heard the rumble of a volley. We came out of the forest into cleared fields and saw there a ramshackle little building, from which some dozen Hessians were fleeing for their lives. I realized that this was the first time I'd ever seen the backs of our enemy, and, wondering at the sight, trotted on faster. The sleet blew in clouds across the fields, and through its smoke we saw a larger group of Hessians, drawn up aiming their muskets at us.

"Fire on 'em, the bastards!" yelled Kite, his proper drill commands forgotten. I raised my piece and pulled the trigger, flint struck steel, and nothing happened. Although I had marched with the firelock's pan wrapped in part of my blanket, it had got wet and was useless. Not so Jib's piece; he fired, and there was noise and smoke. For an instant he stood stock-still, holding his firelock a little in front of him, smiling at it in amazement. Others were firing, and though the distance was too great for the shots to have much effect, the Hessians, seeing themselves outnumbered, jumped up and ran, having discharged a volley that did us no harm. I glanced over my shoulder to see what had dislodged them. It was indeed an infernal sight. Behind me hundreds of men were boiling across the fields, screaming and shouting, the dirty remnants of their clothes flapping; it looked as though the dead had with dumb and common impulse leapt from beneath the frozen clods to seek their revenge on the living.

The Hessians fell back on Trenton, and we followed

them. I became aware of distant firing and realized that the other column had gone into action from the river road. Our depraved scheme seemed to be working.

So we came pell-mell to Trenton from the west side of the town. I saw once again the pleasant frame houses past which we had fled three weeks before. As we clattered toward them, I heard the boom of a cannon, mournful in the storm, and hoped that it was ours. We crashed through a listing picket fence, ran across a back lot, and came to an alley where we could see one of the two main streets that ran through the town from north to south. Our surprise must have been complete, for Hessians were still tumbling out of houses, some pulling on blue and red coats over yellow waistcoats, some struggling to get jackets onto their bare backs. One officer, obviously just come outdoors, was swiveling his head from right to left, trying to ascertain the most immediate source of danger. On the instant, it was shown him, at the burst of a cannon from the top of the street. Grapeshot chattered by, and the officer went down with his leg off at the knee. As some soldiers crouched down to aid him, Sergeant Kite tugged at my elbow. "In there!" he shouted, pointing to a house whose yard we had just crossed. "Dry your piece. Stop gawping — you have no bayonet. Get inside!"

Jib, Malachai Code, and I ducked in through a pantry door and proceeded with some caution through a kitchen. Nothing had been cooked there for a while, but the smell of the place made me homesick for a moment. It was months since I had been anywhere near a kitchen. Beyond was a room that had once been pleasant but had been turned into a shambles by the Hessians. Books with their pages torn out were scattered about, furniture had been broken up for kindling, and one of the occupants had not seen fit to go out into the storm to make use of the privy. Two windows faced on the street, which now was crowded with Germans running this way and that, beginning to form into companies.

"There's nobody here," said Job. "We'd best go upstairs." We did and came into a front bedroom strewn with equipment. "Oh, oh, oh dear God!" cried Code, and I thought that he had been shot. But when I looked at him, I saw him seizing upon a pair of gleaming black boots. "Oh, you lovelies, oh!" In a trice he had them pulled onto his naked feet. "Perfect, perfect!" he crowed. "They might have been my own." He jumped up on the bed and did a little dance, which Jib and I were watching when Sergeant Kite entered the room. "What's all this?" he screamed. "Get to the windows, you mazy bastards!"

"A minute, a minute," I said, scrubbing my piece dry on some bedclothes. Then I charged it and, by God, dropped the ramrod, although Kite, already at the window, did not notice this old sin. I went to join him there and saw on the street a scene of hurry and confusion such as there shall be when the final trumpet sounds. The Hessians were still striving to form into companies, but Knox's guns kept clawing them apart. Officers were shouting and waving their swords toward the guns, and the men stood their ground. "They're

168

good soldiers," said Kite as I broke out the window with the butt of my firelock. And indeed they were; I know how long Captain Totten's Company of Pennsylvania Militia would have stayed in that terrible street. I lowered my firelock and peered through a dense spume of smoke and sleet, trying to pick a target. My hands were trembling, and the musket danced on the sill. Finally I shut my eyes and yanked the trigger. The powder in the pan flashed against my cheek, and the piece fired, bucking back against my shoulder.

"You came a long way to deliver that, didn't you, Starbird," said Sergeant Kite, grinning and taking aim himself. I could not tell whether my shot had taken effect; in fact, I have no idea whether I spilled any blood at any point during my service, or whether I contributed to the cause solely through my martial appearance. I bit a cartridge, ran it home, and fired into the storm again. While I was reloading, I glanced up through the window at the furious sky. Clouds were streaming by at roof top level, fast as racehorses, and smoke, whiter and thicker, was blowing along beneath them.

Again I took aim out the window, and saw that the Germans had got a cannon out into the street. One man was urging the horses that were pulling it, but almost at once a ball struck the head of one of them, peeling back the hide over a hideous array of white teeth. The horse dropped in his tracks, and soon the other was down as well, screaming and kicking and chewing at a wound in its side. Bent almost double against the storm and the guns, soldiers in their cocked hats manhandled the piece around. One thrust in a

169

charge, and another started to pound it down the barrel. Code, next to me, fired, and the man fell. Another German seized the rammer and finished charging the gun. An officer fired it; the piece boomed out and jumped up on one wheel as the officer gestured another charge forward. It was expensive work, keeping that gun manned. The fire from Knox's battery seemed to increase, and I saw, in the dim light, the sullen sparkle of musketry in the windows of other houses. The gunners kept falling around the piece until the officer in charge had to dash across the street and pull some soldiers cowering in an alley out to work the cannon. We kept up a steady if inaccurate fire on the gunners, but, incredibly, they managed to get off some dozen rounds.

By this time the companies of Hessians had scrambled for shelter behind the houses, and the gunners were alone with their dead in the street. The gun, its hot barrel glistening with melted sleet, fired once more. Then the constant shouting took on a higher pitch, and a disorganized surge of Americans came at the gun. A boy with a sword chased away a single remaining Hessian, the scarecrow soldiers pushed on down the street, and all of a sudden the action had shifted away from us to the south. I drew back from the window; the room was full of cottony smoke.

"Well, boys," said Kite with some satisfaction, "how do you like the war?"

"Much better than before," said Jib, "for nobody was shooting at us."

"We'll remedy that; come, lads, out on the street with you."

170

"Oh, Sergeant," I said, "this is the first dry place I've been at since we left the White Plains."

"Never mind that — you can get dry when you're old. Come along." He paused and added, more in wonder than in pride, "We're going to win this fight."

We went out onto the street, where the snow was trampled and bloody and marked with long brown gouges where the grape had scraped up the dirt underneath. The storm seemed to have redoubled itself while we were inside, and now I could see almost nothing. Misty figures down the street were firing and shouting, but it was impossible to distinguish friend from foe.

I was trying to make sense out of the smoky pantomime when something tugged at my trouser leg. I peered down and saw a young Hessian, hatless and badly wounded in the chest. He spoke incomprehensibly to me and pale pink bubbles formed in his mouth. I knelt down beside him, but Kite pulled me up by my coat. "Leave him be," he said, and led me, Jib and Code through the ruined streets toward the core of noise, which appeared to be moving out of the town.

There was still fighting going on in the streets, and two bullets ticktocked into the ground at my feet. I was pleased to find that I felt neither weary nor frightened, although the utter obscurity of the goings-on around me was distressing. The American artillery was crashing away like the sky falling, but I could no longer tell from whence the noise came.

We passed through an alley vacant save for three Hessian corpses. "There they are!" called Kite.

171

"Shoot 'em, boys!" Hundreds of Germans, who had apparently been driven out of the town, were now trying to retake it. They were coming toward us, and, above the constant noise of American firelocks, I could hear a Hessian band playing a gay, unfamiliar tune. The regimental standards were still held aloft, but the regiment was melting away beneath them. Our boys were firing from windows and cellars, and our enemy's exertions were dreadful to behold. I saw a boy some years my junior, who appeared to be weeping, load his musket and level it at his shoulder. But it was too wet, his piece missed fire, and in a second he was struck and on the ground. As a gust of grapeshot went through the German ranks, the mass of men paused, eddied, and then moved toward us, stepping over their dead. The band played the louder as the Hessian officers, wheeling their swords, shouted and pleaded. But it was no good; the Germans had lost the town, and they could not take it back. Still, their discipline was amazing. They closed their ranks methodically, as gaps appeared, but in closing they became denser and more vulnerable to grape and ball.

By now the storm had rendered their weapons all but useless. They attempted a desperate bayonet charge but in a twinkling lost some two dozen men and fell back again. I saw one of their standards, a lovely affair of white silk and gold embroidery, go down, to be snatched up again at once. Bands and standards were not enough to save this day, though, and a moment later the Germans gave their ground and began to fight their way out of the town.

"That's the end of 'em," shouted Kite. "After 'em now!" We followed the retreating body, which was barely visible in the smoke and the storm, out through the town to an apple orchard, desolate with its wintry trees. Here I saw the enemy again, brought up stock-still, completely surrounded.

Oh, they were fine-looking soldiers, with their dandy uniforms and their great mustaches, but we had them and they knew it. A few more men fell, and then some of their officers lifted their hats on their swords to indicate surrender, and the standards were lowered. Most of the soldiers dropped their firelocks, but a few, in rage and chagrin, struck them down by their barrels so that the stocks shattered.

And there they stood, forlorn in the snowy orchard, while an officer walked forward to take their commander's sword and Jib, next to me, said again and again with great solemnity, "Look at that. Look at that." I remembered the first time I had seen those soldiers, on Chatterton's Hill, and I would like to be able to say that they now seemed diminished to me. But such was not the case; even without their arms, those hardy foreigners still frightened me half to death.

"It's absurd," said Kite, his professional instincts jangled by this spectacle. "We took them. We drove them from the town, and we took them." Then he grinned hugely. "Not a bad morning's work."

"Morning's work?" echoed Jib. "I feel as though I'd been engaged in this wretched chore for most of my life."

"Look at these boots," Code said to a couple of

Virginians who were standing nearby. "I found them back in the town. Did you ever see anything so pretty?"

There was some commotion off to the south, where other German units were still fighting. But it did not last long; the noise died away, and the Grand Army had crushed all resistance in Trenton.

"Where is the rest of the company?" Jib asked Sergeant Kite. Kite shrugged, and we walked back into the town. Soldiers were milling about in the streets. I do not recall hearing any cheers.

We came upon two officers supervising the destruction of some barrels of rum that had been found. An eager crowd was trying to get at the spirits before they were poured away, and here we found Corporal Curran and some of the others. "Get away from that! Get away from that!" Lieutenant Godkin was calling out. "It will go hard with any man I find drunk."

"Hello, gentlemen, and congratulations. It has all gone very well." This from Captain Totten, all smiles and expansive gestures.

General Washington and Henry Knox rode by, nodding to the soldiers and glancing at the Hessian dead. General Washington looked grave as ever, but Knox was laughing and chattering like a magpie.

I heard Aaron Thane calling, "Jib! Jib Grasshorn!"

"Here's Thane," said Jib. "Do you think he'll admit to this being a victory?"

"Grasshorn," said Thane, approaching with what could be called a smile on his sour face, "you'd do well to take better care of this, for I suspect it has some

174

value." He held out to Jib the splendid hunting piece that Jib had lost at the White Plains.

Jib gaped at it in wonder. "Bowen and Horlacher and I were in a house where some damned German had piled up his plunder. Your firelock was there, along with a lot of clocks and teapots and such. I hope the bastard's dead and in hell now."

Some hours later Jib was using his handsome weapon to help march a company of prisoners back down to the landing. The storm had not moderated at all and now blew in our faces. I was exhausted from the exertions of the last twenty-four hours and do not recall much of the return to the Pennsylvania shore. It seemed an endless walk, and I was wearily envious, throughout it, of the heavy coats our prisoners were wearing. Most of them were sullen, but Horlacher, who spoke German, struck up a conversation with one. The fellow, who had no teeth at all, was the owner of a sleek black mustache, which, upon close examination, revealed itself to have been fortified with boot blacking. After a few minutes of hideous gabbling, Horlacher burst into laughter. "Their officers told them that we Americans are in the habit of eating our prisoners."

"And not a bad idea," said Jib. "I should love to feast on a succulent leg of Hessian." He showed his teeth and growled at a red-coated sergeant, who, to Jib's great delight, cringed. "Stop that!" called Lieutenant Godkin. "Remember the dignity of the cause we serve."

Aaron Thane was sure that a larger army than the one we had captured would soon be upon us, but no such thing happened. I lost all interest in the goings-on around me and kept rubbing at the ice that was forming on my eyelashes.

The continuing storm made the passage back across the Delaware considerably more difficult that our previous crossing. When we disembarked, I noticed two men lifting a third out of the boat next to us.

"Asleep — and who can blame him," said Jib.

One of the men turned around. "Dead. Frozen to death."

We walked and walked, and at last I saw my little trough with its wooden planks beckoning to me like the gates of heaven. Jib said something to me about helping to collect firewood. I laughed in his face and tumbled into my pit, where I slept in a black fastness.

11

General
George Washington

I never much enjoyed any awakening during my term
of service, but worst of all was the one after Trenton. My limbs failed me when I tried to rise, my
throat burned, joints I never knew I possessed ached
and stung, and I was sure that death was near. And so
it was with the rest of the company and most of the
army, for very few were up and about that day. The
storm had blown itself out, but the weather was, if anything, colder. Toward noon, however, Sergeant Kite
came by, called out, "Rich spoils, my fighting cock,"
and threw two thick blankets down upon me. They
had, he explained, been taken from a Hessian pack, and
they made a wonderful difference. I wrapped them
about me and slept until late afternoon, when Captain
Totten appeared to read us a general order from Gen-

eral Washington, commending us one and all upon our behavior during the fighting of the day before.

This was all very well, but I had done fighting enough for the rest of my life and was therefore as distressed as Aaron Thane when, with one day left of the old year, we were again paraded down to the landing to cross into New Jersey. There was more ice in the river now, and the passage took longer than ever before, and there seemed little point to this dangerous maneuver. "More abominable damned folly," said Thane, who was now so adept at articulating any and all grievances that the rest of us rarely bothered. "We took a thousand prisoners at Trenton, and heaven knows how many fine cannon, and that's enough. The rest of the army is going home the day after tomorrow, and what's the purpose of disbanding under the guns of the British? They'll want to get some of their own back, right enough."

And they could do it, right enough. However cheering a victory may be, it rarely serves to make an army stronger, and, as I heard Lieutenant Godkin gloomily remark to Captain Totten, we now had only half as many men as when we were chased through the Jerseys. Lee's men had joined us after his capture, but they were not the multitude we had anticipated, and they were shaky and filthy as the rest of us. The attack at Trenton had not made us warmer, nor had it clothed us or given us more to eat. Nor had it lengthened our terms of enlistment.

This last was not, of course, lost on our commander. That afternoon, after parading through the quiet, empty town of Trenton, we were called to attention. There was some ruffling of drums — a dreary, empty noise it seemed to me — and Captain Totten cast his eye over us to make sure we were sufficiently straight and still. Then General Washington rode out before us where we stood drawn up with other elements of our dwindled army in the dusk.

His face betrayed no emotion, as I imagined it would not when he died. He regarded us for a moment, and we could not have been a heartening sight, standing glum in our ravaged little regiments. The twilight was so deep that I could not see his eyes at all. Beyond him shone steadily the first cold stars of winter eventide. He began to speak and was not very good at it. At first he was barely audible; he paused a moment and tried again. He was not one to coax men, nor was his oratory such as could stir and inspire determination in reluctant breasts. Briefly and coolly he thanked us for the good services we had performed at Trenton. He said that he was proud of us, that we had done well, and that we were still needed. This was a crucial time, and if we would but stay six weeks more, we could sway the course of the whole war. He would offer a bounty of ten dollars to each man who would do so. His cloak unfolded to a gust of wind, and he raised a hand to steady his hat. When the wind had passed, he told us that every man who was willing to remain was to step forward a pace. Then he thanked us again, reined around, and rode off to the side to watch the effect of his words.

Not a man stirred. We stood in a dreadful silence

while the wind blew through our mangy clothes. For a full minute there was not a sound. I felt embarrassment and pity of a sort for the solemn man who sat watching the last of his command. He had come a long, bloody, confusing, and dispiriting way to get to this cold riverbank. But so had I, and so had the rest of the army, and that was that. It was someone else's turn now, and if nobody was forthcoming, then at least we would disperse with Trenton adding some luster to our scant laurels. Still, it was not a happy thing to see all those clanging words and bold summertime resolves disappearing like the thin steam of our breath into the winter air.

Of a sudden General Washington dashed before us again and, horseman that he was, had his mount standing still as a stone with no visible effort on his part. He spoke rather more quickly to us this time and, though the wind came up in bursts, steadied his hat not at all.

"You have done all I asked you to do, and more than could reasonably be expected; but your country is at stake, your wives, your houses, and all that you hold dear. You have worn yourselves out with fatigues and hardships, but we know not how to spare you. If you will consent to stay only one month longer, you will render that service to the cause of liberty, and to your country, which you probably can never do under any other circumstance." Trenton, he went on, was a bold stroke, but no more than a successful raid were it not followed up. Though there had been difficulties with our pay, he could assure us of our ten-dollar bounty because — he paused a moment, then went on — he would supply it out of his own purse. He was silent for a second and then attempted a smile. Let us take our last cast at freedom — a month only would suffice — and then home with all the blessings of the future upon us. Could we bear to waste all we had striven for, waste it for the sake of a few days of comfort? If we could, none could understand it better than he, and his thanks to us for what we had endured.

There was no sweet cozening tone in this, nor was there contempt or anger. There was simply a vast, dignified entreating. He hurried up a little at the end: "We are facing the crisis which is to decide our destiny." He shifted in his saddle, opened his mouth again, closed it, and rode off once more.

I had just heard the richest man in the colonies asking me a favor without implying any threat. Today he is a brave face with lots of jaw, a fine example, a man sanctified. It is hard, at my age, for me to peddle my tales of the War of Independence, but all I have to do is to mention General Washington and people want to hear about our talks together. Well, that was our talk, and I said rather less than he. When I relate the story, my listeners are polite and thank me and move off disappointed that the General and I did not exchange confidences and philosophies over a barrel upon which was unrolled a map of the Jerseys. No, there was nothing like that; just that speech in which he did little more than repeat what he had said a moment before.

When he was through talking, I did not mull over my place in our struggle for independence. A sore had opened upon my lip, and I teased it with my tongue. I

181

licked at it and thought of a couple of words I had exchanged with a prisoner on our way back from Trenton. I had been walking along behind Jib, prodding the enormous German next to me with my musket not so much to keep him moving, for he was docile enough, but rather to keep myself awake. He was bulky as a cask, and all the fine strappings and leather bindings of his equipment made him bulge like meat wrapped up in the butcher's twine.

In the boat, on the river, I dozed with my eyes open, and every so often he would bring me awake by making a noise with his teeth. I'd turn on him, and he'd shake his head in an innocent way, and I'd doze again. When we arrived on the Pennsylvania shore, we walked along together. Halfway back to our camp we passed a stone farmhouse with some ugly trees in the yard and acres of snowy fields behind. A farmer was standing in front of the house, holding a little girl on his shoulders, though there was nothing to obstruct her view of us had she been standing on her own stubby legs. The German looked at the farm and the barren fields, and turned to me with a horsy smile. "You, friend," he said, "you have a God-damned nice country here."

That's what I was thinking about while Washington waited there in the dusk for our answer.

Then a man in another company said, "Oh, hell," and stepped forward. Three friends of his stepped forward and then, to my surprise, Corporal Curran did, and Paul Bowen, and Malachai Code in his new boots. There was a general jostling, and I stepped forward, too. I heard a honking noise behind me and turned to see Sergeant Kite take hold of Aaron Thane's ear and pull him up a pace by it. "There now, Thane," he said, "we scarce could go on without your wisdom."

When we were through shifting, I looked over my shoulder and saw only a score of blue and naked men, spread out down the line, who could not go on anymore.

That night and the next day witnessed the loudest and most strident of all Aaron Thane's complaints. He hardly slept for his rage and nightlong condemned with great eloquence the irony of being pulled by the ear to fight a war whose ostensible goal was the establishment of freedom. "Leave, then," said Jib at one pause in the tirade, but Thane would not; perhaps he was stayed by Lieutenant Godkin's threat. Sergeant Kite was in high good humor. "Couldn't get along without you, Thane," he said once or twice, "though your natural modesty would never let you admit to such a thing."

Even Godkin was amused by this sport and joined in it. "Yes, Thane, without your doughty presence, we should be driven as autumn's leaves before winter's blast."

The next day the intense cold broke, and a warm, springlike breeze blew up. With it came torrents of rain, which fell on us in hatfuls and turned the ground into a soup. "It's a nice selection of weather they offer a fellow in this part of the world," grumbled Jib, huddled in his streaming blanket. All around us, men whose time had run out, and who had elected not to stay on, were gathering their possessions together. They were going about it quietly, with no laughter or skylarking. One of them saw me watching him and felt compelled to defend his action, though I had made no accusation, "My wife was sick when I left, and that was in the spring. I have had no word from her since we parted. For all I have the knowledge of it, she is dead, my home burned, and my crops rotted in the field. I have a son, and he's a likely lad, but not yet twelve years old. I have fought the war from Long Island to Trenton, and that is fighting enough. It has not been an easy service, but I have borne with it and have discharged my obligations to this country. Now I am going back to my family. Good luck to you." He took up his pack and went to join some of his comrades who were also preparing to leave.

By the end of the day, all who were leaving had walked off into the rain. Among those of us who remained, there was a growing concern about the ground we were holding. A little to the south of Trenton, a creek called the Assunpink feeds into the Delaware River. The army was ranged along this creek, with the Delaware on its left. That was fine protection for our left flank, but the right trailed away into nothing in some woodland. The woodland might have sufficed, save that the Assunpink was not much of an obstacle. We held a bridge that spanned the creek at the left of our line, but there were any number of places where the British could ford the stream and pour down upon us, dislodging our right and forcing us around until we were fighting with our backs to the Delaware. Then they could kill or capture us at their leisure, for there would be no retreat from that situation; our boats were all miles upstream.

There was no question that the British were astir, either, for we had heard rumors all day long; Cornwallis was coming for us, and here we were in an untenable position.

Toward dusk we heard heavy firing, and Mercer's brigade was rushed down to the left of the line, where the British were already arrived, and attempting to force the bridge. But the bridge was narrow, and our artillery commanded it. Day had almost fled, so that the flashes of the firelocks showed clear and our cannon shot brief columns of flame. Where the grapeshot struck wide of the bridge, the roiled water was queerly white. At length the firing dropped off and the British withdrew, leaving quite a few of their number lying on the bridge, their pipe-clayed crossbelts glowing in the last of the daylight.

There were some cheers from our ranks when the attacks ceased, but not many. We knew that this attempt had been nothing more than a device to test whether the enemy would be better off taking us tonight or waiting until morning, when he could cross the creek and dispose of us in daylight.

In darkness, a cold wind added to the discomfort of our trapped army, and the ground began to congeal under our feet. At length our every movement made faint snapping noises, as we disturbed the frost that was forming. "Here's luck, lads," called Kite. "We'll be dead of the cold before they come for us."

"We'll not die of the cold," replied Captain Totten, cheerily. "This is a cold army; it knows the cold."

"What's he so happy about?" asked Thane.

The wind blew and blew until we were scarcely talking at all, and the ground was hard as slate. Earlier the fires of our enemy across the creek had seemed vaporous, but now they shone steady as the steady stars.

"Our British sergeant is right," said Thane. "Tomorrow they'll walk across that stream and gather us up like firewood."

"I hope there's some shooting," said Jib. "I'd hate to end this campaign with you alive, Thane."

"Caw away, Grasshorn; you'll make a nice corpse for your mother."

We were in foul tempers, despising one another, and gathered all together around a fire, full of dread. After a while a big dunce walked out in front of us and began hitting the ground with the flat of a shovel, yelling, "Hoo! Hard ground! Dig in, lads, let's see you work!" He scooped up a stone and rattled it around, shouting all the while. Then he dropped the stone and swatted it. "Deeper," he screamed, "and we'll have 'em fair in the morning!"

I watched him cavorting and thought on how I had seen more madmen than sane since I had enlisted. There were always mazed creatures about, sticking their faces into mine and performing some nonsense or other. The trouble with this army was that you could only tell the mad from the sane by speaking with them. From officers to drummers, all looked fit to wear bib and bells. Here was another madman, who would not have had the appearance of lunacy except that he was thumping the ground with a shovel. He flailed away and the cold ground rang to the blows, and then two other madmen came forth and began building a fire out away from everyone, where it would do no good. They got some kindling burning and threw on big logs, shouting, "Cold night! . . . Warm your bones with this blaze! . . . More wood!" and similar nonsense.

I had never yet seen madmen acting in concert (unless all of us who were participating in this campaign could so be called), and I wondered about it. "Do they start out crazy, or get crazy once they're here?" I asked Jib, who, busy chattering his teeth, did not reply.

Once in a while one of our guns would sound a flat and sour note, sending a random ball into Trenton.

While I watched the antics of the ground-slapper and the fire-builders, I heard a stirring behind me and turned to see a cannon trundling by, its wheels muffled with rags that were laced to them. The gunners pushing and prodding the piece said not a word. Behind the guns a column of men went forward silently, and then we too were being ordered to our feet. "Up! Up!" called Sergeant Kite in a voice that, being a whisper, was well-nigh unrecognizable as his.

"What's all this?" boomed Thane, and Kite fetched him a hearty knock on the side of his head. "Shut your bleeding mouth, you bastard," our sergeant said, whispering still. We formed into a column and stood waiting for five or ten minutes. Ensign Bryce passed our short ranks, and Malachai Code asked him in a low voice what we were about. "I've no idea," said Bryce, "but we're to be quiet." It was easy enough to be quiet: since the wind bit the deeper when we were standing, we stood with our heads sunk between our shoulders and made not a sound.

The man with the shovel had subsided, content now to walk in small circles, when a murmurous sound ran back toward us, and we started forward. Behind us there was a large but quiet jostling noise, like the ocean heard from afar, and I realized that hundreds of men were on the march.

"Oho, it's not so daft," Jib said, as we passed by the two men who were feeding the useless fire. "They're sent to make our enemies think we are still here, when we're going to be somewhere else."

"That's right," said Ensign Bryce, his voice startling me, since I had thought him up at the head of the company with the officers. "We're stealing a march on them."

"I'm glad this fire tending is not Godkin's concern," said Jib, "for he would see that we were at it until daybreak and then have all thirty of us attack across that creek."

"Keep a civil tongue in your head," said Ensign Bryce, and immediately gave way to a giggle. Recovering, he said huffily, "I imagine you men think it's good sport to ridicule a man who wishes to engage the enemy."

"Ensign Bryce," said Jib, "I have not enjoyed good sport in some time. I would like to know where we are going."

"I do not know," said Bryce.

No more did I, and soon I did not care. The march on Trenton had been fearfully bad, with its winds and weather, but this one was worse in its way. We were dry, but we were deadly cold and knew not what we were about. The ground was hard by now, else we could not have negotiated a hundred yards, yet the road we traveled was a poor one, thick with tree stumps which brought the cannon to sudden halts. When the guns stopped, so did we, bumping up against one another and dropping our firelocks.

At first the trees about us creaked in the wind, but soon the night became so cold that they stood still as wrought iron. Every now and then there would come a loud cracking noise, as a tree, in freezing, split a limb. At one of these explosions there was a scuffling behind us, and I heard men running away. The noise subsided, and we went on, stumbling over stumps and ruts. Every so often a halt was called, and each time we resumed the march, a few men would bump into others who had dozed off standing up. Eventually the wind dropped entirely away and the only noise in the black night was the creaking of gunwheels and the shuffling of feet. At length I lapsed into odd waking dreams, clear little images that would float before my eyes for a moment, then vanish. I saw a stain on the wall of my home that had for no particular reason terrified me when I was a child. I saw Mrs. Collins' wise, weary face. I saw my father fiddling with a watch and was overwhelmed with a foolish pity for the man. That pity quickly transformed itself into the very similar feeling of homesickness. I longed for my room with its unsteady washstand and the hideous picture of a little girl embracing a goat that had hung on the wall for as long as I could remember.

At last the cold earth again began to turn its face toward the day. I could make out snowy fields and woods about us. Then, as we crossed a small creek, the sun came up, and all around us was radiance. Every fencerail, every hedge, every twig was sheathed in a chrysalis of hoarfrost, and the light flashed at us as from a multitude of prisms; one could almost hear its frigid glitter. I wished my father could witness this intricate landscape, for his watchmaker's soul would have rejoiced in the sight.

"Oh, that is lovely," croaked Jib.

"I know this place," said Ensign Bryce. "This is Stony Brook; we must be marching on Princeton."

And so we were. In a little while we were halted, and a man from another company came by with a couple of buckets of rum, which was most welcome, for we felt even colder now that we could see the frosty world. The man who had brought us the rum had a word with Captain Totten while we were drinking it. Totten nodded and addressed us: "All right, boys, we're going to take Princeton today. The bloodybacks have got the front door locked, but we're going in the back. That road over there leads off behind the town. Our boys will run in and the British will run out, but they'll have no place to go. We're going off with Mercer's men directly, to destroy a bridge over that creek we just crossed."

We fell into line and marched on toward the bridge,

about three hundred of us, while the rest of our force left the main road for the smaller, cruder one that ran behind Princeton. I could see General Mercer up ahead of us on his horse, and walking beside him, speaking with him, was a familiar figure. It was the burly officer who had sent us up to Chatterton's Hill that October day two months before.

"Why, that's Colonel Haslet," I said. "But there's no sign of his troops."

"The Delawares' time ran out, and they went home — what was left of 'em," said Captain Totten. "I expect Haslet will be off to raise another regiment after this campaign is over."

But Haslet did no such thing, nor did we destroy the bridge, for everything came unhinged.

We were still some hundreds of yards away from the bridge when a messenger galloped up, standing in the stirrups and beating his horse. He said a few words to Mercer, who gave out some orders. We swung off the road into a field of slippery, frozen wheat-stubble, all of us wondering what was happening.

"Look," said Jib, and I turned to see a British dragoon watching us from his horse on the crest of a ridge some distance from us. "Riflemen, shoot that man!" shouted Mercer, but the horseman galloped off before anyone could get off a shot at him.

"They've seen us now," cried Captain Totten. "Come along quickly, lads." With the rest of the brigade, we trotted toward an orchard whose bare trees were spiky against the bright sky. We were halfway through the orchard when we heard a volley, and at the same instant a scattering of twigs, cut by the balls, pelted down around us.

"There they are, by God," said Kite. There were about fifty of them, and it was happy for us that they had fired high. With much shouting of orders, we spread out into a line and moved forward. I fired my piece and reloaded it as we went. The enemy fell back before us. "Easy work, men," called Godkin, laughing.

"Oh, Jesus, look now," said Thane. We had come to the northern edge of the orchard and there before us was a British officer, fine as could be on his brown pony. A couple of spaniels barked and frolicked about the hooves of his horse, and behind him stood an entire British regiment in line of battle, their bayonets glittering brighter than the frost.

I went all prickly at the sight. "Pour it on 'em!" called Captain Totten. One of our two cannon fired first. The gunners were loading with canister, which made a horrible squeaking noise as it went through the air. I fired again and loaded again, staring at that steady red line and thinking the idiotic thought that I had not eaten since the day before. We did not get off more than two volleys; the smoke from them rose in a single beautiful cloud into the still air. The British fired once and then leveled their bayonets and charged us. There was no standing against it. We were ordered to retreat, but we were already running when the order was given.

The British were out for blood that day. They were upon us and among us, and they were savage. Aaron Thane stumbled and fell, and before he could regain his feet, one soldier had driven a bayonet into his spine and another, eyes burning with bale-fire, dealt him a slice to the neck that half took off his head. I saw Colonel Haslet grab his face and fall, and right after that, I passed a Virginian officer who had eight or ten men standing in formation. "Gentlemen," he called, with absurd Virginia punctilio, "dress your line before you make ready." "We will dress you!" shrieked a soldier, and shot him dead.

"Stand and fight! Stand and fight!" This was Lieutenant Godkin, standing all alone, sword drawn, looking not toward the swarming field but to the sky. He was directly before me, shabbily noble with his long nose and steadfast stance. My shoulders itched with the imminence of having iron between them, but I remembered that pathetic poem he had written to encourage us, and I found myself staying my flight and taking him by the arm. "Run! Run!" I yelled in his face. "They're killing everybody!"

He gave me a dazed and angry look. "You would flee St. Crispin's Day?"

"Please, please come away." I tugged at him with one hand, clutching my firelock in the other. He would not come. Angry and, I think, weeping, I babbled about our weak strategical situation, and begged him to save himself for a better day. None of this took very long, and halfway through my pleading, a tiny British soldier came upon us. I swung my piece at him with my left hand and felt it bounce lightly off his back as he stabbed Godkin so fierce a stab that it lifted him off his feet. Blood spilled from his mouth even before he fell.

193

His assailant had to brace his boot against poor Godkin's chest to withdraw the blade. I ran, watching the
withdrawal of the bayonet over my shoulder, and now I
stumbled. As I picked myself up, yet too numb to be
panicked, I saw General Mercer's horse go down. Not
far off, the British had one of our guns and were bringing it around to bear upon us. I dashed across the
clanging field, which sloped gently down toward a
fence. There I caught a glimpse of Sergeant Kite, facing the enemy with his musket clubbed. He dealt a
British soldier a blow to the side of the head that
cracked open the man's skull. Then he scrambled over
the fence, with me close on his heels. The wounded
were wailing and screaming, our own guns had opened
upon us; and I heard a voice behind me yelling, "Rebel
scum!" again and again.

Beyond the fence the ground rose up again in a low
hill upon whose crest I saw trees and a great many men.
Thinking them British, I stopped so abruptly that I
again lost my footing. Then I realized that they must
be American troops, and, sobbing, I started for them.
They seemed to be waiting on the crest but as I approached, most of them turned and ran.

They were, I learned later, Pennsylvania militia.
They had never been in action before, and this must
have been a fine first glimpse of it for them: cannon firing in their faces, dead men strewn out across the field,
wounded writhing and shrieking, and those of us who
were left retreating toward them at a dead run.

I made the top of the ridge and found pandemonium

there. Officers were trying to get the balky Pennsylvanians back into line, which the men were not disposed to do. Grapeshot strummed by overhead, everything seemed to be exploding, and I felt that death was upon me. I was making for the rear when I was grabbed from behind and swung around. It was Sergeant Kite who had collared me. Captain Totten, who was standing next to him, had lost an eye; he had been slashed from forehead to cheek, and the hideous wound opened and closed as he spoke. "Come along, Starbird. Get into the line."

"There is no line," I squeaked, crouching down.

"Get forward or I'll kill you this minute." I was, for the moment, more frightened of Totten than of the British, and Sergeant Kite got a few of us moving back over the crest of the hill. Here I saw the enemy, reformed after their chase, making ready for a final charge to finish us off. They were dressing their ranks in their cool, dreadfully ominous way. Opposing them were, here and there along the ridge, a few of our men who had been bullied forward by their officers. Some were firing; others merely cowered there, waiting for a chance to slip away. My firelock was charged, but I was frozen with the irrational fear that, should I fire it, I would be singled out for particular vengeance by all those tidy red-and-white soldiers who were soon to be upon us again. "Fire, you bloody farmers!" yelled Kite, and I discharged my piece straight up in the air.

Jib appeared beside me, wide-eyed and dirty, clutching his weapon. Before I could congratulate him on his

195

escape, the enemy, all straightened out, began to stir. "Here they come," said Jib.

"Let 'em come!" called Captain Totten almost gaily, standing up and showing them his fearsome face.

They stepped toward me, and I heard, to the right, the explosion of a cannon. I saw half-a-dozen British soldiers go down, and looked to see two of our guns, out forward all by themselves, quickly and skillfully worked. Whoever had command of the pieces knew his business, and that was good, for at the moment, those two guns represented the entire armed might of the Grand Army. It wasn't very much, but it was enough. The two cannon banged away, and the British ranks hesitated for a few awful seconds.

"Freelon! Freelon!" Jib clutched my arm and pointed beyond the guns, and there was General Washington on his white horse coming toward us at a full gallop, his aides laboring to keep pace with him. Behind him came our troops at a run, holding their firelocks before them. Washington plunged in among the fragmented Pennsylvania militia, exhorting them. I saw him leaning down in the saddle, calling to officers and men, and shortly they began to return to the hill. As Washington rode opposite us, Captain Totten grandly lifted his hat to him. "Parade with us, my brave fellows!" shouted the General. "There is but a handful of the enemy, and we will have them directly."

At last we had a line of men standing on the ridge, and we began moving forward. When the British were not thirty yards away, General Washington rode out a few paces ahead of the line, turned to face us, shouted "Halt!" and then "Fire!" There was a noise louder than artillery as our whole line fired and, at the same instant, the British replied.

There's the end of General Washington, I thought as the gout of smoke obscured him. But when it lifted there he was, still in the saddle, steadying his horse with one big hand and waving us on with the other.

"That's the game, lads," called Kite. "That's it, you beauties. Now fire!" Americans were coming in on the right, forming and firing like veterans, and I stood in the line with Jib and Paul Bowen beside me, firing and loading, firing and loading. Smoke was all around me, so thick that I could see little pink fingers of flame in it as firelocks went off along the line. I could not tell whether we were still being fired upon, could not see the British at all; but then there was a rent in the smoke and I glimpsed the enemy line, still intact but moving slowly backward.

"Charge 'em! Charge 'em!" screamed Kite, and we went in after them. For a moment the British split apart, then re-formed around their artillery. And then they were not an army at all, but just men in red coats running away across the field as fast as they could. For a moment I was neither happy nor excited; I merely felt a vast, dumb surprise.

Sergeant Kite showed me what looked to be twice the human complement of white teeth in his smoke-blackened face. "There they go," he said.

I looked away from them and marked the wonderful

fact that General Washington was smiling all over his most inexpressive face. Spurring after the fleeing British, he cried, "It's a fine fox chase, boys!"

"On 'em, lads!" called Captain Totten, and I ran forward with the others. The next instant the cold morning air dealt me a blow and I was on my back gaping at the sky, whose deep clarity was a bit rubbed here and there by remnants of powder smoke. At first I thought I had fallen again, but when I tried to regain my feet, my left leg gave out. I felt no pain at all, but then I looked and saw that the leg was most dreadfully chewed up near the knee and bleeding freely. Already there was blood all around me, pink where the snow had sopped it up. I rolled onto my stomach and watched my friends chasing away from me. Despite his wound, Captain Totten was bounding along. Jib was pausing to drive home a charge, and Sergeant Kite reached out an arm to clap him on the back as he trotted by. I wondered why my leg did not pain me, and then it did. It burned hotter than fire, and I screamed and whimpered and bit my tongue and eventually lapsed into unconsciousness.

12

Mrs. Collins

I was taken to a gristmill, and awoke before I arrived there. The vivid Princeton sky came and went away again, and for a while I was in a wagon with a man whose nose had been shot clean away; he kept trying to speak but always choked on his blood. "A ball in the knee is what happened to me," I said in reply, and then kept saying it for the rest of the ride, since the litany, once spoken, pleased me. I felt the blood throbbing in my leg, and imagined it was spilling away, but I had the grace of sleepiness to draw death's sting. There was some firing in the distance; I was calm in the knowledge that it was no longer any concern of mine.

I had no such pleasant torpor in the gristmill. I was on a stone floor, cushioned by a fistful of filthy straw. My leg pained me damnably, and the men about me were screaming all the time. Once a man crouched over me and whispered, "I don't mind, for it is not all the way off." He raised his arm to show me a hand suspended from the wrist by only the most slender strip of skin.

He went away, and a surgeon arrived beside me with a bottle of rum in his hand. He winked at me, bent over and sniffed at my leg, and said, "It has to come off; hold him, boys."

Two men in leather aprons grabbed me, one by my shoulders and the other by my good leg. I protested and the surgeon said, "Easy boy, it must come off; else you'll die." He took another tug at his bottle and leered at me.

"Leave it alone," I cried, "for you are drunk."

"And so would you be," he said, "if you had this task to amuse you. Take some of this." He handed me the bottle, but I gagged on the rum. "All right then, boy," he said, "you'll have it cold. It could be worse; you might have had your lights tampered with." He produced a knife dark with old blood and held it between his teeth while he selected an instrument from a box. "Saw," he grunted, and branished something whose application I would have thought to be cabinetry. He put it to my leg, and I shuddered at the chillness of it. Then he took it away and put his face close to mine. I could smell the spirits on his breath and was surprised by the wonderful roundness of the tip of his nose.

"What's your name?" he asked, and I told him.

"Well, Freelon," he said, "you will sure not like this, and it will hurt. But do not disturb yourself with my

200

competency. I take the spirits to keep me awake, not to dull myself. Your friends have been coming in hurt for days, and I have had a deal to do. But I know this work, and you will recover. Cheer up, you hero; after this last fight, the British surgeons have more of a task than I."

He took my leg off, and I screamed and swooned and woke to stare at a distant lantern that smoked and stank. I cried for water, but nobody brought me any.

Afterward I had the fever and saw shining insects walking near me on tall, thin legs, and had not the strength to cry out at them. There were men lying on both sides of me, and their elbows hit against mine as they squirmed in their sorrows.

At length two men stood before me where I lay, and one said "We are taking him away."

"I cannot release him on my authority," someone else said and the other man said "Your authority is a fart in the wind to me, you little squit." The two men lifted me up and carried me out into the daylight; the brightness of it pained me as my leg did. So I was taken away from the mill in a drover's wagon. My father and my uncle had come for me, Jib having got word to them.

The rest is soon related. I lay again in my own room, feverish and unhappy, and received a visit from the same slender and elegant physician who had tried to save my mother, although I cannot imagine how my uncle contrived to bring him down from Boston in those troubled times. He fussed with my stump and said that there was little else he could do; the leg had been nicely cut off. He went away, and my father came in with a pitcher of water and the gold watch, which, he said, was truly mine. I have it to this day.

When I was a little stronger and had begun to look forward to the appearance of the milk and broth that was my fare, it was one day brought to me by Jib. He was very thin and haggard, and brought in on his coat some of the cold of the out-of-doors.

"Oh, Jib," I said, "then you have survived it all."

"Yes, Freelon, the whole company is home now, and Captain Totten is busy raising another. The army is in Morristown, and they're colder than we were the night before Princeton. I'll never be that cold again." He laughed and took my hand. "I see in the *Gazette* that the British just had a big celebration up in New York, for their officers. Fireworks and the like. But they do not have much to celebrate."

My father opened the door and told Jib that the finest physician in America had begged that I not be excited. Jib grinned and told him that the finest physician in America could not know much about excitement, and left.

A day or two later my uncle appeared, resplendent in a captain's uniform. My father fluttered about us as we talked, speaking again and again of the strain of folly in our family. "Freelon," my uncle said, "you have brought all the good advice I gave you after that nonsense at the State House to nought. This war may be folly, but it is the less folly for your blundering actions than it might have been. How can I let a milky little toad like you send Britannia cringing back to New York

202

while I sit on my arse here? That fat man Totten has secured me a company, and we cannot do much worse now than I did up at the Lakes."

"Jonas," said my father, "leave him now, for he is weak."

"Weak, is he?" said my uncle. "Well, perhaps, but a month ago you had all your watches buried and were waiting on the word to flee the city. Then Freelon and his noisy friend Grasshorn and some other babies employed a strange alchemy, and now there is not an enemy in the Jerseys. I had best move at once, or your legless son will have me at a disadvantage for good and all."

He went off with his command and was killed the next autumn, helping Greene with the rear guard at Brandywine. Not long after his funeral, the British were everywhere in Philadelphia. By that time I was tottering about on the wooden leg which now gives me less trouble than my real one. Philadelphia was not so infected with the cause of liberty that it refused its conquerors a handsome welcome. Polly Lycott was part of that, and I chanced upon her not fifty paces from my home. It was a murky autumn day, there was water in the streets, and her companion, a British officer, was taking great care to direct her around the puddles. She spied me and threw a pretty hand up to her pretty face. "Why, Freelon, I had heard you were home and was desolate that I could not pay you a visit."

I felt a residual anger but, I was happy to note, none of the old longing. I suppose that I smiled at her, and I suppose that it was an ugly smile, for she gave her companion a beseeching look and he said, smirking, "I am sorry to see that you have suffered some inconvenience."

"Better to have it shot off than to dance it off, you perfumed pimp," I said. The injury we were discussing prevented him from striking me down, and they passed me by. Polly came to no bad end; when, after a grand ball that she attended, the British left the city and the Americans came in from Valley Forge — they came in from that place walking like soldiers, too — she was as cordial a hostess to them as she had been to their adversaries. She married a Continental officer and bore him a dozen children. My old rival Sligo Consett fared no better with her than I had, to my considerable enjoyment. Moreover, his father had been so ostentatiously happy with the British occupation that he was forced to leave the city when it ended. Sligo went with him.

For all my father's certainties of doom, he did well with his watches throughout the war, ever thinking his moderate success was a jape of the gods, who would soon destroy him. But instead it was the quiet, ironic Death perched on the clock near Queen Elizabeth, who finally took him — and, perhaps as a reward for my father's servitude, took him sweetly and gently.

Before that, when the battles swung away to the south, I took myself to New Jersey, to the cottage of Mrs. Collins. I came in the spring, as one should when engaged in such errands, and found the place shuttered and still. Near the doorstep a dog twitched in its simple dreams and did not stir as I knocked upon the door.

Mrs. Collins let me in. She looked older than I remembered, but she laughed when she saw me and said, "Why, it's young Starbuck."

"Starbird," I said, and, after hearing the welcome news that her Tory husband had died in some Jersey skirmish, I wooed and won her.

My father was distressed when I brought her home, for she seemed the living image of my uncle's wife. Unlike that unhappy woman, however, she throve on childbearing, and the number of my children and grandchildren is now at least as great as the number of men with whom I stood at Princeton field.

It is, in fact, her son Peter who will soon relieve me of my watchmaking duties. He has turned out as steady as my father, whereas my own children have done all manner of things. My daughters married and stayed in Philadelphia, but one of my sons embraced banking, prospered, and moved to New York, another fell under Jib's vile influence and became a ship chandler, and yet another, a lively boy but something of a wastrel, has gone west.

I think them all mad, in their way. The banker, for example, is putting inordinate sums of money into trans-Atlantic steam navigation, a foolhardy project if ever there was one. Yet most of the uses of the world now seem mad to me, even in Philadelphia, and I suppose that is one of the penalties for living too long.

As of two years ago, Sergeant Kite was still alive. He kept a smithy at the other end of the city, and every six months or so I'd go over and see him. There were always men lounging around in his shop, spitting on the floor and such, and though he would deride me before them, he was happy enough to see me. He stayed in the war right along and was there at Yorktown when the long files came out of the besieged city and surrendered once and for all. I would like to have seen that, but not enough to have endured the campaigns that led up to it. I asked him about it once, and he said, "Don't worry yourself, Starbird. We had the Frogs with us then, and the poor King George's men were tired. There was music and all, and I received the thanks of a grateful nation which did not wish to disdain my services by the mention of money. That is, I think somebody read something thanking us, but I'm not sure. You and Grasshorn went home after Trenton and Princeton — the smarter you both than me — and those were the fights that mattered. Most of the boys went home after that, but there were always a few men left who had seen the Hessians throw their firelocks away and the British regulars break their lines and run. They never forgot it."

I've been meaning to go see if Sergeant Kite is still there, but I'm not as lively as I was a year ago. I am still working with watches, though my stepson Peter catches me up on small mistakes now — not often, but more than he should. He saw General Washington once, though he does not remember it. The street was crowded, so I lifted him up on my shoulders and he saw him right enough. General Washington was dead and in his grave by the time my youngest was born. I remember the man better than Jib does. My old friend has taken to telling folks that, one winter when he was bringing wagons of food to the starving American army at Valley Forge, he saw Washington praying in the snow. But I can tell you that that brave errand of mercy was something he never mentioned to me at the time. When I challenge him on his Valley Forge stories, he fidgets and says that he likes to relate them "for the edification of the young."

I remember those days better than Jib does, though he is good company and I am always glad to see him. He thinks the work we stumbled into is all done; I am not so sure of that. Already there are a lot of fussy laws that seem part of an old tyranny to me, and with our flexible government a tyrant can ascend to the throne without even the grace of heredity.

But I am far too old now for that to be any concern of mine. When I wonder, I wonder about the past.

I have often asked myself why, when we saw those hardy, long-legged Massachusetts boys — who were, in the end, not fools, and who had seen enough of a war to know what the chances were — striding away together across winter meadows at daybreak, we did not follow them. I never have come up with a satisfactory answer. More and more, nodding over some familiar watchmaking task, I have seen beyond the gleaming curls of metal those desperate roads that led to the Delaware. There wasn't much to keep us walking them, and yet, for all of Aaron Thane's complaints, for all the hopelessness of our cause — and make no mistake about it, it was hopeless — not a man in our company went home until his term was up. We had lost one battle and seen a bigger one lost for us, and there was no indication that we would suddenly do better. And yet every morning, when the remnants of the army woke up and straggled along pursued by the British, our company got up and straggled along with them.

I paid some attention to the Napoleonic War. Now, that was a war: the British brought scores of thousands of men against Bonaparte, and Waterloo must have seemed the end of the world to those who were there. Imagine a whole countryside in flames! In the biggest fight I was in, I was always aware of trees and lands undisturbed not far away. Any solid farmer has twice as much land as we fought over at Princeton field. Yet something happened on that poor little lot which, I suppose, will echo down the years louder than the noise of Waterloo. I may be prey to an old man's visions of the grandeur of his youth, but this America seems to have a great bag of canals and steam engines and mountains and such, and every time I see a new map of the country, it is nothing like the one I saw a week earlier. Europe still looks pretty much as it did on the maps of my boyhood.

So, to finish this up, I would say that perhaps we contained within ourselves a purpose beyond any knowledge we had of it. And perhaps, more simply, we realized that since those soldiers half a day away from our backs were part of the greatest military effort in history, they were there for good reason. If the king and his ministers threw so much money and so many men into the pot, they did not do it glibly; they were in for high stakes. If they thought us worth the effort, then maybe we were. "They never have sent this much stuff to India," Sergeant Kite told us once. "You men may not think you can make much trouble, but they do; they're sending out their best, on a winter campaign. Come on, Grasshorn, step along. Stir your bones, Starbird; you can lie down when you're dead. Walk, you lazy cows!"

So we went on, held together, I think, by our enemy's appraisal of us.

One of Aaron Thane's popinjays, Thomas Jefferson, has told us that good wishes are all an old man has to offer his country or his friends. As this is doubtless the case, I will now close my narrative, sending you all the good wishes I have at my command. You did not have to walk the road to Trenton, but I did not have to endure a reminiscence of it. If you feel, then, that my efforts and yours balance one another, it will give the greatest pleasure to

Your obedient servant,
Freelon Starbird